THE MIGUEL YARULL DOMINICAN DREAM

and other stories

Miguel Yarull
The dominican dream and other stories

La Pereza Ediciones

Miguel Yarull

The dominican dream and other stories
© *Miguel Yarull*
Original title: Bachán: Catorce Cuentos del Montás

© Translation by Achy Obejas

© First published 2024,
La Pereza Ediciones, USA
www.lapereza.net

ISBN: 978 -1-6237523-8-5

Graphic Design: Estudio Sagahón / Leonel Sagahón
www.sagahon.com
Cover and book Julián Herrera

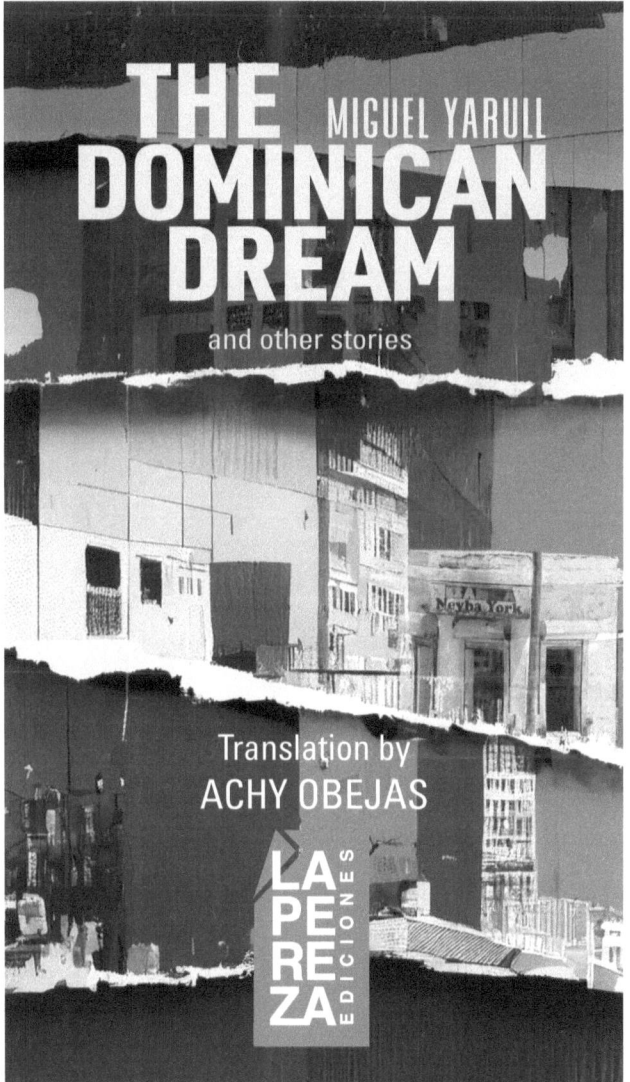

THE MIGUEL YARULL
DOMINICAN
DREAM
and other stories

Translation by
ACHY OBEJAS

LA
PE
RE
ZA
EDICIONES

This book was translated
with the collaboration of
Lorgia García Peña
and the
University of Princeton

THE DOMINICAN DREAM

At barely three in the morning, the line snakes down the block.

Across Manhattan, in the comfort of his apartment, Marino Moquete turns around and huddles under the blankets. He still has six hours before work. The air conditioner kicks in, picks up, lashes out at the last stretch of night.

Outside, New York slowly dawns. Everyone knows they won't move a step until eight-thirty in the morning, but order is paramount for entry.

By sunrise the line has doubled. By seven o'clock in the morning, three hundred Americans have gathered around the consulate. At this hour, Marino Moquete finishes watching the news from his country on the

Spanish-language channels and calmly rolls out of bed.

His day has begun.

After a typical breakfast brought to him every day from Caridad Café, he adjusts his tweety-yellow jacket over his tightly woven shirt, counts the six gold rings on his fingers (three of which spell his name in syllables), checks his briefcase, kisses his wife goodbye and leaves to represent his country as the Dominican Consul in New York.

He's calculated the route to work to the second. By the time he goes up 180th Street at eight fifty-five, he can see part of the throng that gathers every day to make document requests.

Five hundred people anxiously await the decisions of a man in a bottle-green Caprice Classic. On the stereo, Zacarías Ferreira helps him warm up with a few bachatas. Every day, the future of these Americans rests with Moquete and his judgement, which seems fair most of the time. The car goes around the consulate to the back gate. Jimmy, a priggish blond the embassy assigned him as a driver, pulls forward into the parking lot under the eyes of federal security guards.

At the gate, two American guards await the Consul and greet him respectfully. Marino gives them a slight nod as he walks toward his office.

In the hallway he glances at Manola, a secretary from Santiago who's been driving him crazy; she works for the vice consul. He drops his hand on her waist and plants a kiss on her cheek. Manola can't do anything but smile at him and Moquete is glad to be the boss.

Before he gets to his office he takes a look through the one-way mirror. There are more people than usual. Poor souls. If they only knew not a tenth of them are going to walk out with a visa. But the process isn't free, and in the meantime, for every American who applies, Mr. Consul gets the crumbs.

Life is beautiful.

Moquete's office is something else. A carved mahogany desk from Santiago, made by an artist from Licey al Medio is the main attraction. Marino also asked for five red suede armchairs (covered in plastic, of course) to be included in the move, as well as three watercolor paintings of roosters, his diploma as patron of the "Liga de Softball de La Otra Banda," and a framed photo of of himself dressed as a firefighter from the Villa Alta-gracia substation.

A *yaroa* delivered from a diner owned by a guy from Moca, in San Nícolas, is waiting on his desk. Moquete immediately digs in as his greasy fingers leaf through the day's correspondence.

Outside, people suffer.

First in line is Reggie Jackson, like the ballplayer. A strong, hard-working black man who got in line at eleven o'clock the night before. Jackson brings a sheath of documents that prove he has a life here in the U.S. and he doesn't intend to stay and look for something better in the DR. From bank letters to commercial references, this man from middle America had to do some research for his appointment with Moquete. He's been sitting on the sidewalk for almost ten hours waiting to be graced with favor from the Caribbean Caesar.

Behind Reggie, a pretty blonde named Bar-bara visits the consulate for the fourth time without success. She's brought her youngest child with her because she has no one to leave her with at home. She's a stockbroker in New York, but she's sure that somewhere on the island true happiness awaits. Hope is the only thing she hasn't lost.

Like them, there are five hundred more waiting to pay two thousand Dominican pesos to play the great rejection lottery. Whether they win or lose, they have to pay and ask God or the patron saint of travelers to light their way.

The forms accumulate in piles for Moquete, who robotically reviews them at an accelerated pace. He already knows by heart what to look for to so much as give them a chance.

Jackson, Reggie. American. Social Security number. Blah, blah, blah. Dark complexion, a little odd, short on cash. No family there but even fewer here. He collects unemployment and Social Security. You're screwed, Reggie. We don't need problems in the DR, we need solutions. Go rot and come back in two years.

Next.

Jackson, Barbara. Blonde. It'd be good to get a piece, but she has even more deficits than Reggie, because she's got family in the DR. Her sister is a Jehovah's Witness and goes on missions to Constanza. She must think you're an idiot if you believe she's really going on vacation. What she wants is to stay. As if the country had enough to share with these raggedy gringos. Strike four, Barbara. Two thousand bucks and come back in five years.

Next.

The voice brought Marino out of his reverie.

Mouh-quetei.

Marino stood up and walked to the window.

Mouh-quetei, Marino. Yes, sir. Your petition for a visa has been denied again. Please wait two years and try again. Thank you.

It came clear through the loudspeaker, as if for everyone to hear.

An executioner's voice, cold and amplified, confirming all his fears.

A mix of shame, rage and impotence crowds Moquete's face as he tries to compose himself, straightening his tweety-yellow jacket, picking up the three folders filled with papers describing his life, and saying goodbye to the rich man with whom he had stood in line and who would surely be given a visa for fifty years. He adjusts the six rings on his fingers and takes his two girls by the hand, because he didn't have anyone with whom to leave them at home.

He blows his nose with a handkerchief and steps out into the scorching sun at the intersection of Maximo Gomez and Cesar Nicolas Penson to try and catch one them shitty shared cabs that would take him anywhere, away from the shame he felt, and give him back a sliver of dignity; a broken down car that would pick him up from the dirt he now laid on and wipe away the dust and sadness that covered him; a shitty cab that'll swallow him up and spit him out into the bowels of a country that has nothing more to offer, while he regroups and figures out from which beach he will launch the raft that would take him away from the failure that is his life.

SPORTS BACK PAGES

MELANIE
Cobain's girlfriend

Melanie got nailed just before she went out that Friday night, when Fernando finally got her. She looked like a punk princess. Her mother, Marina, insisted on taking it because Melanie looked just like her when she was seventeen, back in sixty-nine, back when people were just starting to smoke weed in this country, like in the States, and Marina was always cool. That's why Melanie (who was originally going to be named Janis) had to pause and pose before going out and spreading her legs for her boyfriend of just six months.

Melanie had been a beautiful little girl. She grew up among Zeppelin records, Tra-

volta's *Saturday Night Fever* and Allen Gins-
berg's poems laced with thousands of untrans-
lated cigarette butts. Marina had exposed her
to everything, and Melanie absorbed it all.

They trusted each other right up to the
moment when the girl had her first joint. On
that upper-middle class teenage night, Fernando dealt out the fun. The moment they
met, Melanie knew she'd do anything he
wanted.

The night in question she'd made herself
up imagining she was Cobain's girlfriend,
Marina even helped. They'd shared a glass
of wine while listening to "The Crystal Ship."
They talked at length in half-truths and, when
she was ready, she said goodbye.

The photo was processed at one of those
Foto Colors between Lincoln and Lope de Vega,
with 24-hour service and Express Pick-up.

The roll also had photos from a trip to
Terrenas Marina had taken with a group from
work, one of Kiki the parrot, and one of Melanie
and Marina, the kind where the camera's
right up to your face and you shoot.

They'd both stuck out their tongues at
the same time.

ZEFERINO.

Or El Zafiro.

Zeferino de Jesús Almonte. Dominican. Occupation: privately employed — who knows what other crap the application asked for. He swears he once washed cars at San Pedro Park with Sammy Sosa.

A Dodger scout gave him his first opportunity and so he started practicing at the sports complex. His age wasn't working for him so he got his papers in order and shaved eight years right off. That's when he was called up. He was well aware he had to look the part so he was meticulous when he shaved just before he left. Got himself a jacket and a shirt from a neighbor who rented out stuff for quinceañeras and wakes, and skipped the cockfight and the night clubs to give himself a whole night off, just like he'd heard Sammy had done when his turn came up. The camera blinked: Zafiro — that's what the loudspeaker at Yankee Stadium would call him — had made it: He looked like he'd just turned twenty-two instead of thirty.

But it wasn't his fate to get out of that damned hellhole. A treacherous shoulder, motherfuck. When that fine American named Carl or Carlos clocked his best 75-mile fastball in the summer of 2002, Zafiro went back to being Zeferino de Jesus Almonte and the second 2x2 in the little envelope was delivered to Quica, his mom.

They were instant and Zeferino posed alone.

... TIENE QUE SER LA MEJOR

They managed to get to the community center where Rufino worked. He'd only been there eleven months and, even though he'd started as a house messenger, he was given more and more responsibility all the time. It was a Thursday and about sixty people came. Rosalba's family, who lived in Samaná, stayed for just one night, its members spread out to all the homes of the people they knew in the *capital*.

It was his second marriage and her first. In spite of the hardships, Rufino got a case of Barceló Añejo, a hearty stew and a beautiful pink dress Rosalba wore with much grace. It was like one of those dresses from the Brazilian soap operas Rosalba loved. Dresses that became popular because women could let their tits hang out without anyone asking them to cover up. When it came to music, a local band was asked to play until the national electric company or the center's emergency back up blew up.

The photos were taken with a very modern camera owned by Julito, Rosalba's cousin, who made his living that way. It wasn't one of those thin ones that look like a toy, the kind people take with them on tours to Boca Chica or Poza de Bojolo. This one had a case and a bunch of accessories. It came with a tripod so the photographer could focus and position everyone before taking the pictures; it also had a built-in flash, the kind that lets you skip waiting between photographs, those few seconds when people are getting ready. It was a real plus for Julito, given the heat in that club.

The shot in question is the best of the thirty-six Julito delivered in a beautiful album, with a dove on the cover and everything. It was almost eleven o'clock and things were heating up. The drunken singer began "Ese diente de oro" and the cake was brought in. Rufino and Rosalba intertwined their glasses and gazed into each other's eyes, madly in love. They looked at the camera and flashed a big one. Then *beso, beso, beso* and flash, another one.

Rufino wore an elegant tuxedo with a red bow and a rose in his lapel. Very handsome. There wasn't a better one among the other thirty-shots. In most, they were either wiping their sweat or surrounded by people or one of them had their eyes closed. It's worth noting the famous one in which they're kissing, framed by the back window of the Skoda, a loan from Rosalba's uncle, the owner of a spare parts store in Haina and best man at the wedding.

Unfortunately, it was out of focus.

EVERY YEAR, THE SAME THING

Carmela Santiago had eleven children. A matron, if you will. She was very serious in the 2x2 taken for reasons nobody remembers anymore.

Her children don't know if there are other photos from that day, but they don't think so.

ALEJANDRO D'AGOSTINI

Allesandro Armando D'agostini Mera was born in Santo Domingo on March 27, 1933. A respected businessman, Don Alejo, as he was called by those close to him and by all those who had the pleasure of knowing him, was a true gentleman.

A man of the world, a staunch fighter against the dictatorship, a man with a vast general culture, an incalculable fortune and a humility atypical among his peers, Don Alejandro spent the last years of his life between wine and philanthropy. His glass and tobacco empires were in good hands — those of the the third generation by then — and come autumn it was his and Doña Tati's turn to showcase their grandchildren and their good manners: old money, as they would call it in English.

Although there are thousands of photos, there are no photos.

ME

I don't know what I should say about myself. I'll just describe myself at the time. We had just gotten up and it was very early. Too early now that I remember how much we had drunk the night before. I imagine the morning light was favorable. The light is flattering every morning in Jarabacoa. Ingrid took the photo. Somehow I was revealed in that piece of paper. No excuses and no pretensions. I'm so glad mommy chose that one. I would have too.

Of course they had to cut it because I was shirtless. Naked. It may sound poetic and pretentious, but that's how I came out: naked.

I was happy.

Purely happy.

It's difficult to describe happiness. That photograph made me happy. I don't know if the other folks on this page knew happiness, but for a moment, during that short click, the girl I liked the most managed to capture my happiness on a piece of paper.

Today I take up about 4 x 5 in this morning paper. Right between Melanie and Don Alejandro's three (none included a photo, but they ranged from family to foundations). Above us was Doña Carmela's, sparse like every year. Below that, Rufino, but just his face.

Just to the right of the Major League scores, Yankees vs. Texas to be precise, Zeferino continues to curse his shoulder as he has every day since he lost his contract —although lately the curse has extended to the redneck truck driver who took him away while he drove a scooter with no lights, just nine days ago, as it reads in the caption below the photo.

GLASS TABLES

Fuck.

The conference table has a glass top. God oh mighty. You can control yourself. Of course you can. Look straight ahead the whole time. People's faces are the key. You know there's a lot to see underneath but it's not ideal. Maybe ideal is not the word: it's not wise.

Mr. Hernandez has the floor. I hope this meeting ends quickly, that this guy next to me doesn't feel compelled to show off when it's his turn to speak. So far so good, I take notes in my notebook and try not to look down. What Hernandez is saying is very valid. Transportation systems in this country need to be optimized. The fuel savings would be something... something... something... something as paramount as the precise way that pink slipper fits Natasha's beautiful foot, dangling right here in front; those perfect wine-red painted toes molding to the tightness of the tips, resting one on top of the other, temporarily stacked, sacrificing themselves for a greater purpose. Her white skin, smooth, moisturized for sure. Then she moves her foot about an inch and her toes settle, flirting, opening and closing the little in-between slits, until she rests again. I'd like to take off that slipper and put my... stick my whole foot in... for God's sake, man, for God's sake. What's the matter with you? You're at a regional meeting. Come back down to earth, it's gonna be your turn soon and this is important. Concentrate, nobody cares about your condition.

(Although the word condition is very unfair when I have everything under control, as the doctor assures me).

Notice how I'm able to turn my full attention back to the vice president of purchasing, who is now talking about imports and the implementation of a new accounting system that will help us enormously with the new tax reforms, and that interests me since I work very closely with monthly invoicing, but not as closely as I would like to work Melissa's feet, now peeking out from under the glass, to the right of my folder, partially wrapped in black leather heels, toenails black, all black. The bitch has pulled off one of her shoes and gently strokes the soles of her feet with her other ankle, as if tickling herself, amusing herself a bit and forgetting about this annoying world where you have to work instead of spending the day licking your coworkers' toes until you faint from pleasure. At the end of the table, where everything is boring, the guy finishes up with a little Robin Sharma-like self-help tip that everyone applauds but which, personally, sounds like bullshit to me.

Osvaldo takes the floor. Osvaldo is a nice guy and we get along well. He works in inventory and he's proposing a new way to speed up dispatches. Sounds very interesting. But never as interesting as Doña Nancy's mature feet. She's sitting in a corner, and I struggle to catch a glimpse. Those feet have walked many a carpet, have been softened by stones, and are encased in white heels with thick border lines. Those feet have self-respect but still cry out for a little sicko to give them what they deserve. That's a French pedicure on those nails, as it should be for Nancy, who has all the money in the world and the feet to prove it. Surely her husband has never caressed them and, if he has, it's been a formality while watching TV and rubbing them because he had to, because Nancy's feet lack satisfaction, yes, they're beautiful but unsatisfied. Then there are those big, well-defined toes, ready to be sucked or to make me... Domínguez, dude, for God's sake... pay attention. You've got a hard-on, man. Get a hold of yourself. You're at the regional meeting. Osvaldo is almost finished and soon it'll be your turn.

Check your notes. The index cards should get you back into the meeting. Stop screwing around and concentrate, all the big guns are watching you. You're already on probation after the January losses you didn't report on time. January is never a good month and that's part of the argument you're going to use right about now, as soon as this asshole next to you shuts up and it's your turn. And as soon as that happens you drop your notes and have to bend down to get them. You don't know if it was an accident or intentional, but the fact is you're down here now, where you should be. A breath away from Natasha's feet, a step away from Melissa's, within arm's reach of Nancy's. Then you realize the glass didn't do them justice. You confirm that Natasha squeezes her toes as if she were cold, as if she wanted to be under a blanket, doing it in a hut, naked but wearing slippers; Melissa continues to play, but now it's both feet she caresses, rubbing them with the plush of the carpet and feeling that tingling that goes up to the last hair on her head; Nancy discreetly opens her legs and shows you the soles of her heels while rocking them on their tips and you can't take it anymore. You haven't been able to take it for a while. From the moment you walked in and saw the table had a glass top, you knew what this was going to lead to. You knew you'd have to run to the bathroom just like you've been doing every day since you joined the company, just like you did at the last meeting when the January reports you weren't able to present were passed around. But none of that matters now. In this place nothing matters because there is no one to judge you. You've shut the door tight and you've silenced the voice that says you need help. You shake your hands and everything gets better. You're no longer sick because you've freed yourself. You just left your sickness on a piece of toilet paper. You threw it in the trash and washed your hands thoroughly.

Now you walk into the meeting room and you're well again. You're ready to explain the February and March losses. You're ready to justify your disability. You're ready.

The jerk next to me finishes his presentation. I wipe away the sweat. I have the floor. Everyone waits for me. I put my notes together. The girl from reception comes in with a tray and eight cups of coffee. She's wearing low brown shoes with half-worn straps. Her even, humble toes with unpainted nails are beautiful to me.

Fuck.

CHAMP
(Surfer Caravela)

Holy shit, champ. Turn that shit up. David Gilmour's monophonic, plucked, pointed guitar punctuates the deep, charged weed smoke in the air, like a wall going up to the ceiling and recycling itself and then swirling around the room until it slowly evaporates.

Pan pararan pan pan pan. Pan Pan Pan Pan. A couple more times. Then, off-key and hopeless, Waters interjects in stereo.

So, so you think you can tell heaven from hell, blue skies from gray...

Shit, champ, Pink Floyd, man. Sooooooo good. That's music, dude. That stuff brings back a lotta things. Lately I'm on a memory kick, champ. Turn that thing up a notch. You know, when Carmen starts haranguing me, I kind of withdraw, I roll up. That chick, man, that chick has me on edge. She just nags, nags, nags all the time. She's like, we have to take the two kids to school, we have to go to the damn Multicentro, we have to pay the electric bill cuz if we don't, they'll shut it off. What a load of shit, champ.

Can you tell a green field, from a cold steel rail, a smile from a veil, do you think you can tell...?

You know how long it's been since I've laid a hand on a board? Two years, champ. Two years! Dude, if you woulda told me ten years ago I was going to go two years with no surfing, I woulda told you to go to hell, brother. You remember when you, Payano and me used to dive in at Boya at the crack of dawn? That empty beach, that smell of wax at six in the morning? Shit, champ. Ripping it up until ten o'clock, on the board, and then, cool, going back home. Not Hawaii, champ, not Hawaii. Hey, man, I'm not supposed to be nostalgic but I'm pretty down, man. Fuck. This chick is blowing up my cell. I'm not picking up, champ. Fuck her.

Did they get you to trade your heroes for ghosts, hot ashes for trees, hot air for a cool breeze, cold comfort for change?

Do you remember all the girls we got with in this country? Shit, man. I counted ten at the same time. That's girlfriends and breakups, ten. And I was pretty easygoing. You started with ten, great. One time, you bagged a cop's little sister, and he got stupid — ahahaahahahaaa. That cop had never been in a fight in his life, that big lazy ass. If they hadn't rushed him away, you woulda killed him, great. Shit, champ, this is how it is.

Did you exchange a walk-on part in the war for a lead role in a cage...?

That's what I'm saying, champ, that we all died and no one's been told. The other day I saw Baby. Listen to this, man. Baby at a video store, a bag of baby bottles on one side and his wife's purse on the other. Baby, on a Saturday night! A guy who crushed any-one who got in his way at Pizzarelli. Hey, because Baby did fight, man. And he did really bang a much of girls — ahahahahahahaha-haaah. That's what my wife doesn't get. She thinks I was born a lazy ass, 'cause she met me on the way down, champ, and now she's got her foot on my neck, man. Look, she is calling again. I ain't picking up the damn phone. I ain't going to no Barney's birthday party with two hundred little kids! I knocked her up when I was already old, man, I know that. But I ain't surrendering. Bullshit. Turn that up, champ.

Gilmour's guitar Solo. Taking his time. With an aimless abandon. Even rockers lose everything. There's dust in the meandering streets of a city in which weed isn't smoked anymore, a city that swallows and wanders about with no lyrics, like a great automaton, dancing to lounge drums, tribal tones, Future Sound of London and glowsticks.

I wake up scared everyday, man. This girl is worse than my old man when he stuck me in rehab. Worse, champ. She goes through everything. Once she found a bong in a drawer of mine, man, and I'd better not even tell you how she went on and on. I didn't say a word, man. Then she starts to fuck with me, saying my kids are already grown up and I can't be fucking with drugs, as if weed was drugs, champ. I didn't tell her I found a couple of Adolfito's pills and I smacked him so hard it even hurt me. Because it's not the same, champ. That kid's sixteen, and it's not the same as when we were sixteen. We knew how to deal with things without getting screwed up. We started when we were thirteen, how could we not know how? Ahahahahahahaha. I did such a number on him, in the end I actually felt sorry for the kid. I had never taken one of those pills before, but I got so crazy —ahahahahahahahahaa. Boy. I was on fire. I hit all the bars. These guys nowadays know what's up, champ. It was six in the morning and I was still staring at the ceiling. I even fucked my wife, champ. Tongued her and everything. After that she didn't let me screw her for two months.

How I wish, how I wish you were here...

Now she's fucking with me about work. First it was about losing weight and now it's about work. I tell her, in this country nobody wants to pay me what I'm worth. I told her I was going to Punta Cana to get some work, to rent boards and she told me what I wanted was to go fuck around with surfing and drugs and women. I mean, she wasn't totally off. But it's true, champ. I studied business for two years at APEC. I ran the stores for the old man until he threw me out. I can speak English. I work my ass off when I have to work my ass off. So, you tell me, am I gonna work for twenty or thirty thousand pesos when, at any moment, I could hit it big with something that'll take care of us forever? No, man. It's best she keep working at the bank until I can figure out something to get us going.

Shit, man. This girl never gets tired of calling. I'm not going home! Today's Saturday. That broad is probably watching Don Francisco. I'm fed up with Don Francisco, man. If I meet that old son of a bitch on the street, I'm gonna rip his head off.

We're just two lost souls swimming in a fish bowl, year after year...

Fuck, champ, it's just all so shitty. That's why I like to drop in here with you for a while, man. It's nice here. Nobody fucks with you here, man. You really got it good, man. You dropped that marriage thing a while ago and you're always chillin'. I mean, being alone isn't easy either, but sometimes you don't know what's best. Shit, fuck! This chick really knows how to nag! I'm going to throw this phone so far, not even scuba divers gonna find it.

Running over the same old grounds...

But, nah, champ. What you gotta do is to take a deep breath and take it easy.

What have we found, same old fears...

Hey, do you know what time Multicentro closes today, Saturday? I'd better avoid more bullshit and buy some dinner and bread for tomorrow, so I don't kill this woman and make my life even more miserable. ...

Hello ... Yes, I'm leaving Marino's house. Yeah, I'm on my way. I'm on my way, Carmen!

...

Take care, champ.

Wish you were here.

THE FRESHEST AIR

Lift your head, Ramón. Lift it. You almost got hit by a car crossing the street and just now you almost fell in a pothole. Lift your head, Autopista Duarte's a dangerous highway. Lift your head, you have to figure this out somehow. That's it: Look straight ahead, don't look down, only crazy people look down. Remember the word, Ramón: God will not let you be burdened beyond what you can bear. But I can hardly stand this. God is going to have to realize I can hardly stand it. Don't lower your head again, you'd better lift it, Ramón. Rest for a while or you'll go crazy, Ramón. That's how your uncle Hugo started, thinking a thousand things at once and now he's tied to a bush somewhere in a field in Azua. So take it easy, Ramón. That's it. There may be some money around the corner, who knows. Problems come and go, but when you fuck up your health, that's it. Rest and look up, Ramón. Your boy is going to get what he needs. Children come with a loaf bread in their arms. Don't think about so many things at once; eat a banana, you still have thirty pesos left and you haven't eaten a thing all day. That's right. A banana won't hurt anyone, and it'll give you the strength to keep looking and show Teresa you'll be able to support Ramoncito, that she won't have to take him to the countryside because you'll be able to support him. I just love that child so much. I love him with all my heart. See, you're building up your strength again. That banana was a good idea. Now rest a while, Ramón. Rest, you still have a long way to go. Why don't you go up, Ramón? Go up for a while, the air is cooler up there. That's right, come closer and don't be afraid, Ramón, you'll be fine. Hugo went crazy because he wanted to. But not you. You're going to get out of this damn streak and you're going to be able to support your family. That's right, keep going up, you're going to feel better. There's fresh, fresh air in the middle of the city. Things will look a little better. But keep going, you're going to be better off. Although I don't think so. Deep down I don't think so. I think I fucked up. I think that damn woman is going to take everything away. But I won't stop. I'll keep climbing because the air here is so much better. Down there, it's just shit. There's nothing. Nothing. A healthy man, wanting to work, and he can't get a job. And Ramoncito, Ramoncito looks so much like me. I'd like to have him here with me. I'd like him to see the city like I'm seeing it. I'd like him to be at the top of this TV station's antenna with his dad, giving his mind a break, telling everybody down there to stay out of my way and to let me rest. Going on the news with his daddy. Telling daddy everything is going to be okay and that he and mami will always be with me.

Always.

KM 29 REVISITED
(Urgently)

The 29th kilometer crossing is dangerous, I thought as the rain completely washed the windshield. I changed the radio station because I was fed up with opinion programs.

Then I accidentally knocked over the CD case. The windshield wiper sped up, but the discs were all over the floor and had to be picked up.

When I got to the crossroad, the rain really started to come down.

Then I cried and they spanked me and I cried some more and opened my eyes and they gave me applesauce which is my fave and they wiped my mouth with a diaper with my name embroidered on it and I pushed the tricycle down the driveway at my grandfather's house in Gazcue and they left me in the nursery and I cried like a little boy and the multi-colored putty got stuck between my fingers and glued to my uniform and they bought me Nacho, a book, and I learned how to write an A and my mom donned mini skirts and wore her hair real high and she was beautiful and my dad had sideburns and pushed me on my two-wheeler but I fell and they smeared something red on me that looked like a mercuro-chrome and it stung and stung and it was so itchy it had to be mercuro-chrome and the bike lost its wheels and I had very, very thick tortoise shell glasses and broke that front tooth when they pushed me while playing Dominican tag but I didn't cry as much as I thought I cried nor as much as I cried when they took me to see Star Wars and Darth Vader comes out again and I cover my eyes tight and can't sleep by myself because Vader's in the closet so I cross over to mami's bed and I sense her warmth and feel safe and my sister's baby teeth are falling out my brother has hair very, very straight hair and Hurricane David blows into Santo Domingo so now everything's dark and everyone's in the same room making jokes that make the kids laugh and feel safe and

the city is razed, full of shattered trees and
for the first time I watch ESPN and it's mag-
ical because in English it doesn't seem like
TV and it never ends and I watch Rocky III a
thousand times and Poltergeist and I fall in
love hard with the movies and it almost gets
hard because Eduardo tells me to pull it and
I pull and pull and pull until I give up because
nothing happens yet but Virgilio tells me to
keep it up that something's gonna happen
and when it finally happens ... I give her a
first kiss which is barely a kiss more like an
obligation because it's about a second long
and nothing happens that's supposed to happen
nor does it look like something out of a soap
opera but I keep pulling on it and now it's
better and like on Cinemax I grab a boob and
she doesn't say anything and I get boob grab-
bing fever and suddenly there's money and
American visas and I'm at Disney World for
the first time and they take pictures of us
posing with cartoon characters and we eat
McDonald's like Americans and a *combo* stops
being a merengue band and I almost cry with
joy because I can take care of myself with my
English from El Domínico which is very good
for a little boy who's gifted a Nintendo and

plays Mario Brothers non-stop papapa papan-
para pa papapapaparanpaparara like an endless CD and they just bought me a drum set
and I feel complete even though I still can't
quite understand that I feel complete but I
play non-stop to a Rush cassette I can't stop
playing modern day warrior of a mean mean
stride which plays for the next twenty seconds
and I play and play and play and play and
then Ozzy and Van Halen follow and the motherfucker who parks cars at Plaza Naco knocks
my Iron Maiden cap off my head because I'm
a little kid and a punk and my mom gets very
happy because that stuff is diabolical boy it's
the devil but with my dad's help I shave my
soft mustache hairs although I know now
they'll grow back thick and my voice will be
thick and at the school chapel I graduate with
a face full of pimples and dying to fuck but I
can't fuck because she dumped me and now
she fucks someone else who's older and I don't
do anything but go to the movies and to Pizzarelli on Sundays and to Neon to desperately
pull up close to any girl when Willie Colon
turns off the lights at four in the morning
with Gitana and De La Paz and everybody
wants to sleep but I want to fuck because

everyone tells me it's worth it and college is better because I finally do it and I study for a career that's not bad while still weighing one hundred pounds soaking wet but everybody weighs a hundred pounds and they don't know what they want but what I do know is I'm a musician a rock musician and I play for pizzas and sodas and now for three thousand pesos and then I put my hand to paper and a song is written and it's not too bad and on stage I sweat and sweat and drink beers when I play and people sing what I wrote and I don't know what to think so I sing along although without a mic because my voice is horrible and I realize drummers don't fuck as much as people think because now it's three in the morning and while everyone else is dipping theirs I'm picking up this damn drum set and carrying it to the car and that doesn't look cool so I can't get laid because it's too heavy and I sweat like a pig and my graduation's at the university courtyard and I still have pimples and the photo with the diploma and my mom who doesn't have high hair anymore and my dad and his belly and my brother who no longer has straight hair and my sister who doesn't have baby teeth anymore comes out in focus after all and I work in an office but they don't respect me because I'm newly graduated and now I drink rum at the Country Club where everyone orders their own bottle and I can afford it but then I throw it up on a beautiful flowered bed at the same club and I still haven't decided what kind of person I want to be while the guys wet my head as I throw up outside Café Atlántico where freaks and gays and straights hang out and I'm sad 'cause I can't relive the night that made me throw up because Café Atlántico is the best thing that's ever happened to this city so I rinse my mouth and go back in and my joy is doubled because everyone is listening I just can't get enough and we jump up and down hugging each other and shouting viva viva viva viva viva everything but please don't yell güebo the manager whispers in our ears to not make trouble and we order tequila and it's like I feel the tequila going down my throat and the burn is shiny and fresh and it's freedom and I'm not so young anymore because I work and have obligations that force me and I force myself and my belly button gets deeper as my belly grows and my hair falls out and I fall in love and I settle in a house with a certain kind of people and I'm already a certain kind of person like all kinds of people who are the same people and the house is big and very beautiful and I get married in the house I mean not in the house but to the house and I get little tired and now I'm tired and I get in the water on a board I'm searching in the waves and find my way and get lost and something happens to me on Playa Encuentro so I lose the board and sit on the sand and what a shame what a shame what a shame what a shame that I don't care anymore because I work and buy things and do things that seem important but aren't important and I buy a car that's not so big but it's blue and fast and I'm driving on the Duarte on a rainy day and knock over the CDs and pick them up and I hear tires screeching and I see the car flipping in front of me.

And just like that, I pass.

ON CHARCOAL

In thirty years, I've never screwed up at my job. I don't have much, it's true, but I've never messed up at my job.

The woman reminded me of a dog after being hit: the black eyes, arms crossed as if she were cold when in fact the police station was infernal. But mostly, it was her submission and fear, like someone who's been mistreated for no reason.

I could've been good. I just needed a push, maybe a gallery interested in my work. But it never happened. The premature family made me trade the brush for a piece of charcoal. It's a lie what they say: Artists don't need to be poor to be good. I never wanted to be poor, especially after Daniel was born.

She sat down, assisted by a sergeant who couldn't quite fit in his uniform. In the ten minutes she'd been in the room she'd yet to look anyone in the eye. Everyone was waiting on her and she didn't care. She looked small, as if the pain of remembering had diminished her.

I can't say I dislike the work at all. Once in a while I do something that brings me satisfaction. A particular stroke reminds me I still have talent. Once, a slanted eye (slanted eyes are always the hardest) came out perfectly. When I finally saw the subject and the eyes, I can't deny I felt accomplished.

They brought her a glass of water and placed it on the table. Her aimless stare saw nothing. It was clear she would start when she was ready. With each passing minute, the silence grew heavier.

The sergeant, in a hoarse voice, decided to step in.

"Whenever you want ..." he said, entreating her as politely as a sergeant could entreat anyone.

The woman didn't answer. The silence doubled.

Rape victims are the hardest. It's painful, but you develop an armor against these things. I imagine the same as a surgeon or a doctor might. The first few times it really got to me; I couldn't sleep for so many nights. But truth is you can get used to anything. Now I no longer see a raped woman in front of me; instead, it's a twenty-minute delay that could make me miss the beginning of the Yankees game.

After ten minutes that seem like ten decades, she came out of wherever she'd gone to make herself comfortable (if you can call that comfort) and announced: "I'm ready."

The sergeant turned on a small recorder on the desk. Samuel took the pad in his hands and wielded a charcoal pen. The woman took a sip from a glass of water.

At last, she'd made up her mind. Let's see if we can get this over with quickly.

"The alley was dark, but I could see clearly."

"Im gonna try to help you, ma´am" the sergeant said, relying on his experience. "How big was the individual?"

The woman looked among the four men in the room.

"Like him." She pointed to the corporal on duty.

"Five eleven, give or take?" the sergeant asked.

"Give or take," the woman said hesitantly.

That's it. We're on our way.

"Good. Okay. What else do you remember?"

"He had black hair, very black. And kind of curly."

Samuel began to slide the charcoal on the paper. The rustling sound of the rubbing accompanied the movement.

I've always been good depicting curls. I like curls. They give some cadence to a portrait. I don't like bald people. They're boring. Curls cheer me up.

"Would you say his face was wide? Was he fat, thick or skinny?"

"Skinny. He was so skinny he looked... he looked like a skull."

She bristled at this memory.

This is going to be good. I like comparisons. They give me a foundation. Sometimes people are so boring. He was fat, or he was skinny, or really skinny or he was tiny. But every once in a while someone comes along and surprises you: He was fat, his face looked like a tomato, or he was so skinny his cheekbones looked like bevels. The skull isn't as good as those, but it gives me hope.

"Good, very good." The sergeant motions to Samuel, who's scribbling loudly on the paper. "What can you tell us about his nose?"

The woman thought carefully.

"I can tell you he was no ordinary guy."

C'mon. You can give me something better than that. "He had a nose like a parrot," for example.

"He wasn't ordinary," the sergeant repeated. "Would I be ordinary?" He was looking for a point of reference.

"Yes," replied the woman nonchalantly.

The sergeant wasn't counting on such honesty and was a little annoyed, though he didn't show it.

"Okay. And for example, Samuel, is he ordinary?" He pointed to the sketch artist in front of her.

The woman looked up. Samuel had been there all along, but it was as if she had just seen him for the first time.

"No, he's not ordinary." She paused. "In fact..." She interrupted herself. "I'd say it was the same nose."

The comparison startled Samuel.

"Good, good," the sergeant said.

He had my nose. That helps. I've drawn my nose a million times. I titled my first one hundred sketches "Self-portrait", the others I didn't care to come up with titles anymore.

Samuel scribbled rapidly. As he drew his nose and contemplated what he was wearing, he paused for a second.

Something had unsettled him.

The nose looked like mine? I don't think so. Maybe she's exaggerating a bit. I'm going to humor her, but I really doubt it.

"We're almost done. With another little push, we'll be ready. What do you remember about the eyes?" the sergeant asked.

"I remember them perfectly," she replied, tightening her mouth. "They were black, but full black. I mean there didn't seem to be any white in them. They were totally round, and he had very long eyelashes."

It's funny how much a person can remember in such a short time, but if there's one thing this job has taught me, it's to believe them. His eyes were round and black, with long lashes, round and black and eyelashes...

The sketch artist, who had just completed the eyes, dropped the charcoal. The sergeant looked at him and saw he was agitated; he'd never seen him like that before. Old Samuel stared incredulously at the woman as he bent down to pick up the lump of charcoal.

The woman looked back at him, and it was as if the whole room had disappeared and they both found themselves in the middle of a deserted stretch of road, just the two of them.

But what is she saying? She's confused. I think we should start over. I should say something. This portrait isn't right.

"What do you remember about the mouth?" the sergeant asked again.

The sketch artist and the woman kept staring at each other. The world had vanished and only their two pairs of long, anguished eyes remained, tied in a knot.

Please, God, don't let her say it. In thirty years, I've never failed at my job. It's the only thing I have left. The last evidence that I've been good for something. I've never screwed up, but if you say anything ...

"The mouth..."

She won't say it. These are just coincidences. She won't say it because it's not possible. One knows one's own, it's just not possible. My hands are starting to sweat, but soon it'll pass. Soon she'll say the mouth looks like someone else's mouth. I have to calm down.

"The mouth..." the woman said again as she searched the artist's eyes for a clue, something to help her say what she needed to say.

I have to calm down,, but I know there's no way out. I know that, in a minute, I'll have to decide. In a minute she'll say it and then I'll have to choose between what I should do and what I have to do. In a minute she'll say the mouth is the same mouth I've known for twenty years. The same as my grandfather's, unmistakable. In a minute she'll confirm the mouth ...

"...was thin, elongated, with white teeth, very white and tiny, as if they weren't even there. The mouth was..."

... thin, elongated, with white teeth, very white and tiny, as if they weren't even there. And then Daniel will be a rapist and I'll have to draw the mouth as I must draw it or make the strokes fuzzy. Let him get away or make him pay. I have to decide now. Now that I still remember the day he was born, the day I held him for the first time. Now that I have to deliver him with the tip of this charcoal pencil. Now that she recognizes his mouth, the mouth that's the same....

"... the same as yours."

The woman pointed at the sketch artist.

CLEAN HANDS

Segundo committed suicide May 14th at ten at night. The poison he took was called *Tres Pasitos*, but his death was more painful than he'd anticipated.

As he vomited blood, he realized his passage to the other side wasn't going to take just three innocent steps and wasn't going to be smooth. Fact is, dying, despite what Eastern religions promote, must hurt.

It hurt Segundo.

It would be necessary to analyze whether his boiling stomach and bulging eyes hurt more than leaving his family how he was leaving them: bankrupt.

Bankruptcy implies there used to be money and now there's none. A panhandler has never been broke. A panhandler might have been screwed all his life. Segundo had never been a pauper and his family had never had to work until now.

Bankrupt. That's how Segundo was leaving his family in this world.

But he had a plan.

THE GOOD SON.

Patricio Ramírez was the second son of Segundo Ramírez and Hortensia Roldán.

He was born in the Cristo Rey neighborhood on October 8th at six o'clock in the evening, thirty years before. His laboring mother managed to kiss his forehead before fainting from pain.

It had been more than five years since Patricio had lost his way.

First, it was the drinking, and then, cock fighting — while alternating with aimless women and sleazy cabarets — that kept him from the right path, but he finally vanished on the first day of November 2002, on his eighteenth birthday. Patricio Ramirez had gone to place bets with a friend and was never seen again. The place was called Rafelito Sport. Five syllables that would haunt him the rest of his life.

ONCE A FATHER

Segundo Ramirez had never been a millionaire. A small furniture factory started in the backyard of his humble home was the foundation of his family's decent life.

In the beginning, things weren't easy. He had to strain to make sure his wife and three little boys had the basics, maybe even the luxury of a hamburger from Los Imperiales on a Sunday afternoon.

But Segundo was a determined man. He'd only had a little schooling, but he had tons of determination. Thus determined, he was able to move his business to a space in Manoguayabo, buy two polishing machines, endless new accessories straight out of the box, and push his ideas and his cojones to get ahead.

It was the early eighties and Segundo Ramírez had taken off.

A FAVOR

It's wise to listen to a man, any man, who decides to put his pride and manhood aside (especially in this country) to ask a favor. The man who gives orders, steals, rips off, makes decisions isn't the same as the man who kneels and asks for a favor.

The day he had to mortgage the three storefronts and ten trucks he'd worked so hard for, Segundo decided for the first time in his life to ask for a favor.

He took the last sip of his after-dinner coffee, put on his business uniform's khaki shirt and went to see Rafelito at the betting parlor.

The place was everything Segundo had imagined. He'd never gambled a penny in his entire life, and the goings on seemed ignorant and dastardly to him.

Joselito recognized Segundo from the moment he walked through the door. He had the same walk as his son. The two men instantly disliked each other, and when two men dislike each other, there's no turning back. Rafelito was a son of a bitch, an opportunist whose reputation came crawling like a reptile before him wherever he went.

He invited Segundo to his office but left him standing. Then Segundo lowered himself, asking him for a favor, man to man: to not to let his son Patricio gamble there anymore. Rafelito picked at his last remaining healthy tooth and wiped his hands with a towel with a motel logo.

"Your son's old enough to know what he's doing," and walked out of the office, leaving Segundo alone in the middle of the room, in the middle of nowhere.

FAREWELL

The funeral was all laments and questions. Murmuring, everyone singled out the son. Patricio didn't shed a tear. Not because it didn't hurt, but because it hurt so much that tears were too pedestrian an expression.

He stared back at those who blamed him and defiantly silenced them with shots of white rum and Montecarlo cigarettes.

Only one other person in the world had known he was sick. The person who never judged or abandoned him. And now that person rested, his lips whitened, in a wooden box he'd made himself in his father's workshop.

A PLAN

The first night the son was too drunk to dream. He tossed and turned in the bed he shared with a whore from Casa Teresa. By the time dawn broke, the pain and bad taste in his mouth wouldn't let him get up at all.

He spent the day smoking, without a drop of alcohol, and reliving his last years. He fell asleep several times. The motel fan spun at the same speed as the night before. Every time he woke, the shock of knowing something was wrong haunted him. Then he remembered Segundo had committed suicide and wanted to vomit.

He fell asleep for the last time at eleven o'clock that night, when Segundo appeared to him.

Segundo caressed his face; he had a child's face. It was Patricio as a child. The tenderness of those calloused hands cheered him as only vice had managed to cheer him.

Segundo asked him to listen, told him he shouldn't be afraid and that he had a plan. Patricio sat on a park bench that later became his cradle and then a horse's saddle. Segundo talked to him the whole time with a smile on his face.

Then three names came out of his mouth: three American League teams.

Segundo gave him a kiss on the forehead and let him keep sleeping. The next morning, Patricio awoke refreshed, eager to get up.

On a piece of paper beside the bed, in his own handwriting, the three teams were mis-spelled on a napkin; the sight split his lips into a smile.

The betting place opened at half past ten. There was time for everything. He walked up 30 de Marzo and had breakfast at Barra Payán. The cold milky juice running down his throat gave him strength and something akin to joy.

He opened his wallet. He had eleven hundred pesos left, that was all his capital in this world. He paid ninety and left a ten pesos tip.

He walked the dirty Villa Juana sidewalks until he reached the door. They'd just opened and turned on the televisions.

Kansas City, Minnesota and Oakland.

A game.

One thousand pesos.

He sat at one of the old tables in the back, trying to blend in. This time he didn't drink. He didn't even look at the TVs.

As he walked to the cashier, he could hear the last out of the last game. He didn't smile or rejoice. Truth be told, he didn't even have to look at the screen to know.

He traded his paper for nine thousand six hundred and fifty-four pesos.

He rolled up the money, tucked it into his pants. When the door to the small office opened, Rafelito's shadow loomed. It made him curious and surprised to see Patricio cashing in.

Patricio Ramírez stared at him. He adjusted his pants, unconsciously tightening the grip on his loot, spat and walked out to the street.

TELL HIM WE'LL SEE HIM HERE

He didn't tell anybody. There was no celebration or waste.

At ten o'clock, Patricio closed his eyes again. At four in the morning, three new names awaited him on his night table. This time Segundo said goodbye with a kiss on the cheek.

It was dawn. Nine thousand. Miami, Boston, Philadelphia.

Two underdogs and a sure thing. Joselito printed the receipt himself.

"Zambrano pitching for Boston?" he asked with a sneer as he entered the data into the computer.

Patricio didn't answer. He folded the paper and put it in the front pocket of his shirt. At five o'clock that afternoon, he had eighty thousand six hundred pesos.

During his lifetime Patricio had lost twenty million pesos of his father's money. Rafelito must have had thirty times that amount stashed away.

One hundred days were enough.

Eight parlors in one hundred days. That was the final balance. Patricio did the math: In fifteen days, he could bankrupt a shop. Father and son worked faster.

On September 8, three and a half months after Segundo's death, two hundred and five plays later, and in total bankruptcy, Rafelito shot himself in the head.

Patricio watched the son of a bitch's wake from afar. When they sealed the tomb with cement, a solitary tear ran down his cheek.

He'd just lost his father forever.

A TWO-FACED TALE

(Beep) "Eduardo. Eduardo, fucking pick up. I know you're there. Eduardo, I'm gonna do it. I can't stand it any longer. Now I'm really doing it. You better believe me. This is the last time you'll hear from me. Eduardo, pick up the goddamn phone, you sonuvabitch.

All right, let this be on your conscience. I hope you can live in peace. Goodbye."

(Beep) "It's her, isn't it? She's who's there. Damn her. And you swore to me you were gonna leave her. How many ways can you fuck me over! I went from being all your reasons for living to being a mess, your weak link. Well, lemme tell you something, Mr. Del Toro, you either are or you aren't, and no matter how much you want to hide it, you know you are, you can't run away from yourself. But why am I wasting my time talking to you? Goodbye, motherfucker. See you in the hereafter."

(Beep) "You think I don't have the courage, don't you? Don't tempt me, I've got it. I'll kill myself, Eduardo! Eduardo, pick up the damn phone! All right, it's better this way. You don't want anything to do with me, I don't want anything to do with life either. Eduardo, my love, I love you so much, please pick up the phone, we can still fix things, things aren't so bad. C'mon, my darling, pick up the phone... I see you're not gonna. I know you're at the apartment. I saw your car there fifteen minutes ago, so you just don't give a damn about this. Don't worry about me, I'll be fine where I'm going. Ciao."

(Beep) "It's not Fernanda, it's your mother, isn't it? She never wanted you to have anything to do with me. Not even when we were studying together, and much less when she got suspicious. Why did you always do what she wanted? Always Eduardito this, Eduardito that. Bundle up, Eduardito, it's kinda cold tonight. Eduardito doesn't go out to discos. Eduardito, thirty years old and still seeking his mama's blessing. That's her. Fernanda is too stupid to even think about it. Too bad your mom still makes the decisions in your life. But I'm delaying my trip by talking to you. I'll leave you alone, mama's boy. See you later."

(Beep) "What did I do wrong? Let's see, pick up the phone and explain to me what I did wrong. I was too pushy, that's what. You never liked anyone fucking with you much, I know, but I can't stand it when I feel you far away, because I always want you near, Eduardito. I'm telling you now: You have been the greatest ... the only one. It took you a long time to realize it, but you have. So accept it, accept that you love me too. Accept me. I'm sorry about Fernanda and the girls, but someone has to pay in this life. I'm going to give you ten minutes to think about it and call me. Ten."

(Beep) "Okay, you're not gonna call me. If you think that's what I deserve, so be it. I, for one, am tired. I'm tired of waiting. Fuck you. Put my life on your tab."

(Beep) "I can't, I fucking can't! I can't leave you! If there's one thing I'm more afraid of than dying, it's never seeing you again. Eduardo, please, I'm begging you, forgive me. Forgive me for being mouthy. Forgive me for having told Manuel, but I couldn't keep quiet anymore. I know that's what's going on. It all sprung from what he said at the party. I could see the horror on your face when Manuel said he couldn't believe in anyone anymore because even the most macho man can turn out to be such a faggot. You were trying to laugh it off and go along with it. I saw how you let go of Fernanda's hand and looked for a handkerchief to wipe your sweat. I saw how Manuel looked at both of us, so subtly only we noticed. I saw his smile, mocking and malicious. I saw how you took it, how you understood my indiscretion; not for nothing are we best friends since high school. I'm sorry, Eduardo, I'm sorry I did it, but it's like they say: If there's no witness, it didn't happen. I had to believe it was real, I had to take it out of our rented studio and make it legitimate. I never believed you all the times you swore that if anyone found out you would kill me. Never, until today, because knowing you're lying in agony on the floor of your apartment with a bottle of pills in one hand and a picture of Fernanda and the girls in the other kills me. That you're not answering propels me to a medicine cabinet just like yours; to a glass of water and ten pills, just like yours; it drops me to the floor and to the end of the tape on your answering machine, because wherever you go, I'll go, Eduardito, I'm telling you even though you can't answer now that your mouth is foaming, now that my pulse is racing, now that our eyes are closing.

WAITING ON A FRIEND

I have never been much of a Stones fan. In my day, I preferred Santana or Three Dog Night, but neither of them had a song that fit me the way this one does.

"I'm not waiting on a lady/I'm just waiting on a friend."

I can't get the melody out of my head. Now that I think about it, yes, it was a coincidence. So many years without seeing her, what would it be now, twelve, thirteen? Meeting her twice in the same week, what were the odds?

I have to admit, there are times when I still worry about what could have been. Twelve years of carrying that little pebble in my shoe, that little thorn in my foot. She looks so much better than I do. It amazes me how the years have not touched her face, taking their toll on mine with the violence of a hurricane.

Vodka and orange juice, as usual, as if not a day had passed. Me arriving early, my old habit; an English quirk in a country that runs twenty minutes late. I don't mind waiting for her, in fact, I enjoy it. It's nice to dwell in the past, leaf through it, dust it off. Funny how time slows everything down. All these years have taken care of that, reducing us to images, to smells, to how good we had it. We would have to dig too deep to revisit the discussions, the lies, the goodbye. Time sells itself as magic and in this it doesn't need modesty.

I couldn't believe it the second time. It was only natural we would have met on Monday in the checkout line at the grocery store, her with her youngest riding in the cart, me alone, with my inexperienced, newly divorced shopping.

Raquel? Adolfo? I knew it was you. Same, you're the same. What's it been? Nine, ten? More, much more. My girl. My shopping. The laughter — the same. I still can't believe it. Me neither. And Armando? Fine, I guess. Your family? All fine, thank you. The silence, the looks were getting uncomfortable. Well, well, well, well. Good to see you. Good to see you.

Take care. One thousand four hundred and forty-nine thirty-six.

The bookstore thing did seem like a sign to me. I've never had time to waste on a Thursday afternoon, but for some reason today I did. Finding her with *The Book of Laughter and Forgetting* in her hands, in that blue dress, unhurried, with time to talk. If that wasn't a sign, then to hell with luck and its sense of humor.

I'm not sure at what point I decided to buy her a drink. Maybe it was right after she asked me about Mario, my brother — two sons, the oldest is already a civil engineer. She said her marriage wasn't going well, that things hadn't worked out as she had hoped, but that she was still married and wasn't sure if a drink would be a good idea.

I understood. Maybe it was true. Maybe there was no need to push it. Surely it was best to chalk these encounters up to the law of probabilities rather than a late encounter with destiny (where did I get these ideas?). So I was surprised to hear myself insisting on the impromptu rendezvous, convincing her it was just a meeting between old friends, for old times' sake, and that, after all, surely at some point in our youth we had made a foolish promise to each other that if we ever found ourselves old and alone, we would have to agree to at least one drink.

Now here I am, in the same bar, with the same drink, waiting for the same woman. If this jacket were leather, and that song were by David Bowie, anyone who walked in would swear it was '84, that Prince had a new album, and Raquel and Adolfo would get married right out of college. "Raquel and Adolfo would get married right out of college." It was all planned, all talked through. Now that I say it and hear myself say it, it sounds as unreal as it did back then. Six months after graduation was enough. She never quite understood why, nor did I bother to explain. It was easier to get going, the scholarship, to move on. How to let her know that, had I stayed, she would have never forgiven me? How to show her I had to leave Santo Domingo, that I had to prove myself alone, that otherwise I would have reproached myself all my life?

Now it's easier. With this vodka and everything wrapped up, everything's easier. But it wasn't easy that Saturday. I never liked goodbyes or airports. It was the last day I saw you in person until last Monday. You were wearing blue, just like this afternoon. I remember you insisting it was only six months and that by the time I got back we would be married. But everything was already played out. I already knew it wasn't going to happen. That it would be first six months, and then whatever it took for this to wear off, for the disenchantment to take over and only then could we move on. Me and my insecurities and you and your life. Me trying everything, looking for questions (because, from the go, I understood I'd never have answers), and you trying to forget, even though you didn't know it yet. You didn't know my phone calls would slow to cessation and my letters would always find excuses to be late.

If it's any consolation, I didn't understand either. I never understood but I didn't ask myself too many questions. I still remember the last call. I was drunk. It was two o'clock in the morning over there and six o'clock here. I got your mother up and, for the first time after eleven o'clock, I asked her to get you.

Then we spoke and I told you four months had been enough for me not to know anything, that I didn't plan to come back for a while, that it was better not to wait for me. I told you everything without even thinking you might be half asleep; that the least you expected when you went to bed that night (after finishing the umpteenth letter of the month) was that in the middle of the night you were going to be left alone, without a wedding and without your two children, with no waiting, no return. You asked, you cried, and I couldn't explain what you had done wrong when you asked me. That was the thing, that you had done everything right, that it was me who'd screwed up, that you were what I was looking for, that when I had you I wondered if there was anything else and that I went out to find it knowing it would never come, that I'd never have it better than with you.

The rest is common knowledge. When I heard about your wedding, I wasn't the least bit surprised. It was always clear to me you couldn't live without giving yourself to someone, that you were the kind of person who could not assimilate loneliness. If it's true that a year wasn't a long time, it's also true that I reaped what I sowed, I got what I deserved.

What surprised me was Armando. I'd never have imagined you together, although I'd never imagined you with anyone but me.

I can't say I had a grudge against him. It's true he'd been my friend for so long, but I could never blame anyone for falling in love with you; on the contrary, I admired his courage in front of everyone. He managed the vows and went further, because he'd had everyone against him. He went on to be the guy who married his friend's girlfriend and didn't care because, I imagine, he had you by his side and that was all he needed.

It took me longer to understand. All these years and a marriage down the drain to realize what I had and what I gave up. A lot of people said you couldn't forget me, that Armando was just a way to not be alone. Today I want to tell you having you like this is still better than not having you, that I think I'm ready for commitment and that we both know you'll never love anyone like you love me. I can tell you that now. I can tell you you've been the only one since I let you go. I can ask you for forgiveness now, and for marriage and a life. Tell you this has all been wasted time. Ask you to let it all go like you asked me twelve years ago. I know you'll accept, as selfish as it sounds, because our story only happens once and it's never too late. I can tell you now, at our table, in this bar of a thousand nights, I can do it while Máximo pours me another drink and tells me a woman called, that she told him to tell me she couldn't come, that it's better this way, that I should excuse her, that I'd understand and that she sounded very much like Raquel, that beautiful girl you were going to marry when you finished college.

RADIO MIL REPORTING

It wasn't always like this. You were very different, Johnny, very different. I remember you as well, as if not a day had gone by, as if you weren't dressed in those rags, as if that bottle of rum didn't take you where it's taken you.

It's been a long time. I'd heard about you but hadn't seen you in almost twenty years. I didn't believe everything they said until today, Johnny. Until now, when I find you in this colmado in Ciudad Nueva with Beltran in the background. Until now, when I look in your eyes and I realize, yes, although there must be something left in there somewhere, in broad strokes there's nothing there: You're dead, Johnny.

If you could see yourself, if you knew what you've become. You'd laugh, old man.

Those were some brisk and rowdy years and you were bigger than life , Johnny. It only took two semesters for the whole university to take notice, everybody knew who you were. Those days were different, a different vibe. You were also different. When you walked it felt like the world was about to change, and when you talked, suddenly it did. You were revolution all by yourself, Johnny: when university was courage you were cojones. Studying law was just an excuse to bring them the fight. Months went by and I never saw you carry a book, and yet you were brilliant.

I've gotta confess, it's hard for me to look at you today, Johnny.

The goddamn motherfucker government and that son of a bitch president. Radio Mil reporting at five fifty, damn it. You tell him, my brother, you're closer than I am. Tell him Johnny Díaz made a promise on his mother's life. Radio Mil reporting, the government isn't going to last much longer in this shitty country, we'll keep on reporting. What are you looking at, motherfucker? Do I owe you something?

Yes, old man, yes. You owe me. You owe me a country. How many times did you lay it out for me. You made it so I believed you. I never let anyone else in, no matter how much they tried to make me see you were nothing but a hot head, a troublemaker, a coward who hid when the police surrounded the campus and then the tear gas and the prisoners and everything else that happened. I believed in you, Johnny. I was nineteen years old and I had ideas, ideas you helped sow, that grew because of your speeches and Aníbal's and Sandrita's speeches.

Sandrita.

I know, that's a low blow: Forgive me, old man. Memories roll over each other and it's hard for me to separate them.

Radio Mil reporting, keep it up, you're going to fuck it all up. Brother, excuse me, you're not going to finish drinking that beer, are you? Thanks, brother, may God repay you. Baní, you heard what the good doctor said, pour one out for me, but make sure it's cold, otherwise the doctor won't pay. Radio mil reporting, there's no electricity nowhere in this damned country.

You ask for so little now, Johnny; how different from what you used to ask for. If you had a beer for every claim you made. I woulda gone on, Johnny, I woulda gone with you to the very end. At least by then I believed in something, even if it was bullshit. Now everything's different, everything's so... comfortable. But you were absolutely right about one thing, you'll never live like them; even if the reasons you offered before are not the same as what's brought you here now, you'll never be them. I know, those memories again.

But I just can't help it, I can't keep denying what I know, old man, because I do know her, Johnny. I know who brought you here, who took your hand that October afternoon and introduced you to your madness. You'll ask me to shut up and I'll oblige. I'll do it for old time's sake. Cheers, Johnny.

Radio Mil reporting, whores are running wild, so much AIDS in this damned neighborhood! Baní, I told you just now it had to be cold, just like the doctor told you. Don't pay for it, doctor, give me another one. I'd like to know who it is you're threatening to kick out of this shitty colmado. Do you want me to set fire to this bullshit? Don't you know who Johnny Díaz is?

Johnny Díaz. If the guy in the colmado doesn't know who Johnny Díaz is, I could explain, although I'd have to ask him which of all the versions he wants to hear, mine or the rest of the world's. Which one do you want me to tell him, Johnny? The one about the hot head from the UASD who, because of too much schooling and his family's economic woes slowly turned into a nutcase who studied less and less and drank more and more? Or the one about the young man who had a future if he hadn't started screwing around with revolution, trova and politics because he was so smart? Or the most epic of all, the one about the rebel who went crazy because of how he was tortured by the anti-riot forces that just loved to play barbarian to our Superman? Bullshit, bullshit. You know it and I know it. You and I know about October, we know about that afternoon and that it was you who should have given the speech at the parking lot. Of all the people in this colmado, only you and I know it was two o'clock in the afternoon and riots were scheduled; only you and I know about the bus that didn't take you to your appointment on time, to meet your bullet, the one gifted to her in your absence, because, at that moment, she was out there saying what you shoulda been saying. No one else knows what she meant to you; no one knows about her twenty years and her dedication, and that you always said Sandrita was your mirror, your forever companion, your sister in the trenches. Nobody knows about the hallway in that dirty stinking hospital and the doctor telling you she'd lost a lot of blood, that they'd do everything possible. Right there and then, you welcomed her, invited her to sit down and make herself at home; by the time surgery was over, her bags were already at your place; your new mistress had found her Caribbean Syd Barret and decided to move in.

And that's it, that's your whole story, Johnny. Right there for anyone who wants to listen. It'll clear up any misinformation any-one tries to pin on the madness. There it is, you can do with it what you want. Meanwhile, I have to go, I just stopped to buy a little some-thing. I left the car running, my wife's inside.

Baní, I'll pay for whatever Johnny drinks. As much as he wants or as long as he can stand it. For old time's sake.

Bye Johnny, see you someday. I woulda loved to hug you and reminisce about those times, let you know how much I've thought about you all these years. I also woulda loved for you to remember I'm not a doctor, I studied engineering.

THE CYNIC

At the Dominican authors shelf, she had no trouble finding it. She took it in her hands and gently caressed the cover. She saw her name spelled correctly for the first time in a long time and felt a sense of satisfaction. She opened it delicately and couldn't help but smile as she recognized the cynicism with which she'd written each recipe.

She looked around.

That whole building devoted to so many books. Some were worthwhile, but most were books about nothing or about sheer BS. She thought about all those authors typing like mad. Some on typewriters, some on computers, the Greeks on who knows what. She could see them, centuries ago drinking wine by the barrel, smoking cigarettes of all kinds, searching in the cracks of the ceilings for the right adjective to best describe a sunset or a corpse.

She imagined each writer's excitement with their final drafts, all those words on all that paper. Words someone had taken the trouble to write, so they had to mean something. Everyone full of themselves, inflated. Then the corrections, the editor and his black pen and his deletions. The deadlines, the printing, the release, the dedications. I have a book: the basic step in this world of literature.

That's why she'd decided on a Lebanese cookbook. It seemed unpretentious and, at the same time, useful.

Although she had the culture and talent to write the great Dominican novel, she focused her efforts on getting the exact quantities of the ingredients that made the Tipile such a feast, publishing without permission the secret recipe her grandmother had passed down from generation to generation.

"Lebanese Food for people who like Lebanese food" read the cover. The title was a little wink at all those folks who spend their lives buying the wrong books. People who fill shelves and shelves with books they'll never read, but which give them a sense of peace and status just by being surrounded by knowledge and learning.

Months later, when the cookbook became a bestseller and three television channels offered her starring slots for a cooking show, she decided to take advantage of her newly acquired fame to write the memoirs of a Dominican with the soul of a Lebanese, who relived her memories daily through the different dishes of her distant country while waiting for the glorious day when she'd finally return triumphantly to her forgotten land, which by that time must have already been buried under the sweaty passage of...

C'mon.

THE BOOK

He had barely begun to read *The Tibetan Book of Life and Death* when his wife sent him to buy bread for dinner. Gritting his teeth, he closed the book, put on his sandals and went out to the bakery. He'd only managed to read the prologue, which introduced the questions the book would eventually answer: How many of us are really ready to die? How often do we think about the exact moment of our death? What comes next? Are we ready to accept Samsara again, to return to this life and follow this chain of repeated sufferings until we become enlightened? What can we do to prepare ourselves to break this cycle?

The book was the first step toward answers to these questions. It was the first step toward spiritual preparation for the inevitable. It was the beginning of a life without fear, without qualms. A life of acceptance and growth, of approaching the light. It was an exercise and experiential guide that would free him once and for all from the illusions that make life a great emptiness, and from the illogical fear of a death that is the only certainty we have.

Too bad he hadn't bought it a year earlier, he thought, as he heard the trigger mechanism the moment he refused to hand over the keys to his truck to the sonuvabitch who had just assaulted him at his front door.

THE ARCHITECT

|| Mr. Ramon Montalvo," announced the secretary's monotone voice through the small device.

He was waiting for him. The appointment had been scheduled for a month. He didn't know the guy, but he wasn't surprised. New clients had been pouring in since the state university's technology pavilion had opened. In their elaborate descriptions, the architecture magazines called it an organic space, with clearly defined environments and beautifully integrated light and acoustics, perfectly suited to its rugged surroundings.

He straightened his coat (he wore a jacket now) and coughed a bit.

"Send him in."

Soon, Ramon Montalvo appeared through the stainless steel and glass door. He seemed older than he really was. Precocious gray hair and wrinkles made him look fifty-something when he'd really just turned forty.

The two men met in the middle of the room, introduced themselves and shook hands. The architect felt a strange sensation as he touched the client, something like a chill on the back of his neck that made him uneasy.

"Have we met?" the architect asked, intrigued by the feelings the man had awakened.

"No, we don't know each other."

The architect dropped the subject and walked over to the conference table in the center of the room.

"Let's see, Mr. Montalvo, how can we help you?"

Montalvo straightened his shirt collar and looked at his fingers as if checking to make sure they were clean.

"I've come to have you design a tomb for me."

The answer surprised the architect. In fact, it caused him a little amusement.

"A tomb?"

"A tomb, a mausoleum."

"A tomb, or a mausoleum?" the architect asked, more to himself than to Montalvo.

"A tomb or a mausoleum or whatever you want to call it. What I need is a place for someone to rest in peace. Let me explain: I would like that person to be buried in a nice, different kind of place. Cemeteries are designed to bring out sadness. I don't know if they're for the living or the dead. I would like what we build to be a little different from convention. I'll leave the details to you. I have plenty of references for your work."

"I must tell you, Mr. Montalvo: Your request is a little odd. In fact, I don't recall ever having designed anything so ... grim."

"No, no, that's precisely what I don't want. People assume solemnity and death are synonymous. And let's face it, nobody wants to die, least of all this person. But death happens. And this person, once dead, deserves a different kind of rest, a unique rest."

"Who is the person?"

"I'd rather not say."

"I need to know something about him or her. We base design concepts on the environment, the personality of the client. And in this case, the client is the deceased."

Montalvo thought for a second.

"Tell you what, architect. For this project, I'll give you complete freedom. The cost doesn't matter. Just make sure the design is pleasing to us."

The architect pondered for a moment. He had been scribbling random lines on a piece of paper for a while now, some of which bifurcated and some of which did not.

"My fees are a little high. I'll have to interpret the project as a residency. Residencies are costly."

Montalvo responded unhesitatingly.

"There's no downside."

"And I'll need an advance."

Montalvo pulled a checkbook from his jacket pocket. The architect was surprised. He was definitely a different kind of client.

"This blank check should cover the costs," he said, tearing it off and signing it.

The architect didn't know whether to accept the check or not. Nothing like this had ever happened to him before. Perhaps this was how famous architects made deals, and he'd have to get used to this new way of doing business.

"I don't need to be paid so soon," he said, trying to seem less hungry.

"I insist. And, yes, I need it to be completed very soon. Fill in the amount. The bill should be in dollars. I trust you." Rising from the chair, Montalvo straightened his jacket.

The architect had no choice but to accept the check.

Montalvo walked away, bidding the architect a simple farewell, leaving him with the piece of paper in his hand, bewildered in a way unfamiliar to him.

That afternoon, he didn't think about volumes or concepts. The architect took his time to do research.

These days, much is common knowledge, but at the time Ramón Montalvo was an unknown quantity. Credit bureaus yielded nothing under his name. Personal references were very vague. He'd been referred by a client whose summer villa the architect had remodeled but the client no longer lived in the country.

At the end of the evening, the architect leaned back in his chair, pressed his fingertips together and brought them to his lips. He pondered Montalvo.

He'd do it.

In this country even death is unionized. When it came time to design the structure, the architect knew from the start only the cemetery's masons could be involved in the construction, and that bothered him. The masons' workmanship wasn't up to the quality needed to complete the project, not with the rigorousness it deserved, but he'd have to make it work.

He decided on a cylinder. He liked the idea that a cylinder had no sides. Like death, it was absolute.

He determined the cylinder should be solid, with no doors or windows or doorsills or crosses. There wasn't much to the design, but somehow it made sense. The finish would be ribbed, interrupted, like life. Exposed concrete and molded lines, he thought.

The dimensions were vital. The proportion of death in relation to life. Metaphysics and architecture met at his desk at eleven o'clock that night. What should be greater, the death of a subject, its physical absence, or the life of the subject itself? How high should it stand? How much more, how much less? He understood a man is measured by the emptiness he leaves when he dies, that few people are recognized in life, and that death is the triumph, that which glorifies or debases it. He decided the mausoleum would be large, larger than the shadow cast by any living person.

Since it didn't have any doors, no one could enter. In fact, it would be built only once the dead had been buried. No one would ever go in or out. An absolute death.

He didn't design chapels or chairs. High in that sad cemetery, the massive white cylinder would serve as a testimony that the afterlife could be pleasant.

The blueprints were ready in three days. The check for fourteen thousand dollars went through without a hitch. The project presentation meeting was brief. The architect showed Montalvo the design with his usual mastery. He suggested materials and gave him an approximate budget. Montalvo only asked if he was pleased with what he had designed. The architect thought about it for a second and nodded.

"It's my best work."

Montalvo smiled, satisfied, then shot him. The architect thought the shot hurt a lot more than he'd been told. Montalvo picked up the plans, leaned close to his ear and whispered something. Before closing his eyes, the architect remembered the project, felt proud again and smiled.

MONTÁS
PROLOGUE

‖ A gun for protection? That's not so hard. What I have most here are guns for protection."

In a dingy room with a desk in the middle, Calima, a dark woman with a bit of a mustache, leans back in her chair and lights a cigar. Her face is partially lit by a small lamp.

There's an old case of beer on the desk.

"But if you got problems, Calima can take care of them for ya. Here on the border, your life is just taking care of problems." When she speaks, she snorts as if she's short of breath.

She pulls a short machine gun out of the case.

"Mama Tingó. This one has the power to take care of anythin' for ya, and fast. But it's not very discreet."

She puts it aside and pulls out a .45.

"Anaísa. A beauty. With this one, you could be in trouble with an elephant and, I promise, you'll be awright."

She rests it on the desk and brings out a silver, shiny Magnum from the same case.

"Liborio. This might be your thing. Won't unfriend you, but the recoil's no small thing."

Calima rummages through the case and finds something that satisfies her.

"Ah, Sergeant, today's your lucky day." She shows him a .22 caliber pistol wrapped in a red handkerchief. "If you truly never want to have a problem again in your life, allow me to introduce you to La Gunguna. This's yours."

She hands it to the Sergeant, who looks it over.

"It looks harmless, teeny, but, believe me, it's killed more people than you've ever met."

The Sergeant hands it back to her.

"Besides the fact that it's blessed, look at the handle, the veneer."

The yellowish gold-plated handle gleams in the lamplight.

Calima points it at the door and, without further ado, fires four times in a row, leaving a single hole pierced four times by the four bullets.

"Here on the border, La Gunguna has been the law for many years. But the time's come for it to walk the earth. So, Sergeant, if what you want is something that'll keep you protected forever, you got it."

The Sergeant sheepishly asks about the price.

"This gun is priceless. You're never gonna be able to pay me what it's worth. But since you're Corbeja's cousin, I'll let you have it for thirty thousand pesos, paying me now."

The Sergeant timidly asks if there's a discount.

"No, Sergeant, I can't give you a discount on something that"ll protect you 'til you die. And I'm getting tired of this. Make up your mind, make it up now or get the hell out."

From the front pocket of his threadbare pants, the Sergeant pulls out several two-thousand pesos bills, counts them and pays.

"Good. That's a good decision, sergeant. No more trouble in your life."

The Sergeant gets up. Calima takes a long drag from her cigar. "Ah sergeant, one more thing..."

At the door, the sergeant pauses.

"Never, ever, let it get wet."

Surprised, the Sergeant takes another look at the pistol, puts it in his pocket and walks out.

"...Pa' que no te jodas."

1: THE FINGER.

He woke up in the middle of a hot, dark Santo Domingo night. He woke up — for lack of a better word to describe getting out of that sticky and sweaty state in which he'd spent the night in that shack in that neighborhood — between mosquitoes and indignation, feeling his sweat like honey and lime sticking to his skin.

He woke up and went out to kill.

It was no easy task to kill a president, but Montás was willing to try.

Three o'clock in the morning seemed the right time to do it. Once, as a very young boy, while he was a bricklayer's helper, he'd been imprisoned for stealing some shoes from a construction site. He experienced prison up close and vowed never to go to jail again. But this city and its darkness were more powerful; so much so that, for a moment, the prospect of killing another man — even if it meant a return to prison — brought him happiness.

It was late, but he felt alive, awake. He whispered to Esther that he'd be back in a while, then groped his way to the door, clothes and shoes in hand. The candles were draining the last of the light from the night, and he felt sick. His determination redoubled as he stubbed his big toe on the concrete block that served to support the coffee table in the living room.

He felt the blood rush and, after a few seconds, the pain finally hit his brain. He cursed the president's damned mother and all his family a thousand times as he lay on the gnawed sofa, writhing in pain and trying to stop the blood, but even then he didn't come to his senses.

It'd be someone's else's blood that would flow, he thought to himself.

Mario Cabrera, a.k.a. El Chino, was a taxi driver. He knew the city like the back of his hand. He worked for a cab company, although late at night he'd turn off the radio and go out on his own. He'd decided he had no reason to hand over what he'd earned with his sweat (because air conditioners in the city, if you weren't in government, was like talking about dollars at the Ingenio Consuelo) to a guy whose only achievement had been to buy a short-band radio, print two hundred stickers and gather an equal number of assholes willing to share their profits with him without complaint.

Lately, he supported himself by chauffeuring foreigners he met at the hotels and Plaza España to get a little sex. The brothels in Santo Domingo were kind to cab drivers and, since he could usually count on the sexual appetites of Spaniards and Germans, Mario Cabrera could make up his last few hundred pesos late at night.

He was crossing Correa and Cidrón, on his way home, when a limping man forced him to come to a stop.

"Whatcha doin'?"

"Still working?"

"C' mon. Where to?"

"The president's house."

Mario Cabrera had gotten a lot of strange requests as a cabbie. When you're a taxi driver, you get used to not judging people by their requests, but the address the man gave him was certainly out of the ordinary.

"What?" he asked in surprise.

"To the president's house."

"Which president?"

"The only one I know of. You know any others?"

He looked at the passenger for a good while, assessing him in the rearview mirror.

"Well?" The man was starting to get restless.

He decided to take him. All in all, there were guards and servants at that house, he thought. Perhaps this guy was starting the early shift in a short while and needed transportation.

Although from what he could see in the depths of that man's eyes, that didn't seem possible.

Puchy was one of those guys with only one name. Freddy, Peña, Jacobo, and a handful of others were known by only one name in this country.

In the capital, Puchy only had one name.

Puchy had been drunk since 1985. He got famous when he drank lamp oil in the middle of an alcoholic marathon, celebrating a City Championship that Licey won against Escogido. He later became immortalized for losing his fear of oil until he fell in a coma. When he recovered, he decided to replace the gas with white rum, no ice, considerably improving his chances of survival.

He was dragging his drunken ass through the streets of Villa Juana at about three in the morning when a cab ran him over.

Montás put on his pants and shoes in the dark. His toe felt swollen now and, as he put on his socks, he thought it might be broken.

He stepped out into the alley and then to the avenue as he lit a cigarette. He made sure he carried the .22 in his front pocket.

As he approached the corner, he saw a cab approaching and flagged it down.

2: THE TWENTY-TWO.

Martín the Stutterer was the best pool player in the world. Compulsive gambler and villain in hundreds of urban legends, Martín operated at Pancho's pool hall in Villa Juana.

Legend has it, Martin once bet a sum of money on a round of billiards, which to date and according to word on the street, reached the heights of one millions pesos.

His opponent was an army sergeant. The Sargent, the name by which he's been immortalized, was stationed in the border town of Monte Cristi for more than five years.

Like any good border patrol, and with nothing to do but fall in love and hone his billiards skills, the Sargent reached ESPN championship levels.

One afternoon in 1998 at Pancho's pool hall, in the midst of one of the longest winning streaks the Stutterer had ever put together, he loudly challenged "any son of his damned-di-di-di-di-di-di-di-di-di-di-di-di-di-di-di-da mother who would like to play with Martín the S-t-tu-tuter-r-r-rrer-r-r, the best pool player in the world, for the whole fuckin' boo-oot-tttt-teeee."

The Sergeant, who'd come to the pool hall by chance and for the first time that day, was a perfect foil. He approached the table, sizing up the Stutterer, and proclaimed he was "son of his damned mother with a purse he wanted to gamble." Unlike Martín, the Sergeant's phrase came out in one breath.

They struck a deal.

They looked into each other's eyes, studying each other, and Martín knew he couldn't lose. He knew it like sniffer dogs know what's in the luggage. They finalized the details while the men at the other ten tables approached theirs, dropping their own games, leaving their beers half full, just to see the show.

"And how much is y-y-yu-your purse?" The possibility quickened Martín's stutter.

"As much as you can handle."

"A hundred? Two hundred?"

"Three hundred, four hundred," the Sergeant said, playing along.

"Wha — five hundred?"

"Five hundred? Well, five hundred it is."

This is where the legend gets a little twisted.

In the language of gamblers, five hundred is five hundred. In the language of that particular pool hall, five hundred meant the winnings were five hundred thousand. Martín, of course, didn't have that kind of money, but a glance at Pancho, retired fucker, lord and master of that place, confirmed that, one way or another, he had his back.

The Sergeant, for his part, had nothing.

At this point it would be good to explain what a border guard earns.

Let's put it this way: The Sergeant, working twenty years non-stop at a post that included some under the table shenanigans, would never manage to scrape together five hundred thousand pesos. You could argue Martín should have made it clear at the time that five hundred plus the purse meant five hundred thousand. It would have been fair as well for the Spaniards to let the Indians know that, apart from evangelizing them, they were going to wipe them off the face of the planet. We'll say Martin decided to use that information, which was known to every man in that pool hall, to his advantage.

The game lasted six minutes. The sergeant asked for a break. He didn't sink a single ball, which meant he'd just used his cue for the last time.

Martin didn't waste a shot. His technique was impeccable, and his courage, hardened by risks and deceit, pumped him up.

And so, when the eight ball finally landed in the corner pocket, the Sergeant's life was forever altered by those six minutes.

❖

Legend has it the Sergeant accepted he'd lost, but he wasn't pleased. And it made sense: He hadn't even had a chance at the table beyond that once. Crouching down, grouping the balls on the table and setting up the next round, he challenged Martín the Stutterer again: double or nothing. "Sure, o-of course. B-but first — show me your money."

The Sergeant, with his freshly cashed paycheck, was offended by the request. In those days, who didn't walk around with a thousand or two thousand pesos on them?

"Look, compadre, there's more than enough money here to play," said the Sergeant, showing him the wallet from afar. Martín caught a glimpse of two thousand and one five hundred pesos bills. But there was a lot of money missing.

"D-d-drop the BS and show me the cash."

"What cash are you talking about, huh? Here's your five hundred and if you wanna keep playing, we'll put the money up front from now on."

In the next few minutes, the Sergeant would find out who he was going to be working for for the rest of his life.

Here's how it worked: Pancho and the other guys had witnessed the bet, which made it valid on the streets. Martín had been working for Pancho for some time, trying to pay him back through labor for a number of gambling debts and other vices Pancho had been graciously financing.

So, by simple arithmetic, the Sergeant owed Pancho the money.

According to the calculations, and supposing the Sergeant gave him everything he had in this world, the debt would be four hundred ninety-seven thousand five hundred pesos.

Not counting interest.

The Sergeant laughed in his face. "Quit messing around," he said, as he tried to pay the five hundred pesos. Pancho came out from behind the counter sliding an old toothpick from one side of his mouth to the other. He didn't carry a gun, but he felt just as dangerous without one.

"No, no, no, no, amigo. The Stutterer isn't messing around. The purse, what you played, multiplies your bet a thousandfold." The silence in the pool hall, as well as a small handwritten sign confirming the rule, confirmed it was all true. He almost fainted as he protested how that could be possible, that this had not been made clear to him, and that they couldn't force him to pay. Sweat soaked his armpits, his back and the rest of his body.

"But we all heard it clearly," Pancho continued, while the sergeant began to realize he didn't owe the Stutterer but the fucker who had a rep for ripping off thousands, millions of dollars in New York and coming to Villa Juana to tell the tale.

"Don't sweat it, bro, though it-it-it looks like it's going to get bad. The only thing we want is the p-p-p-purse. Later we'll p-p-p-play if you want," said the Stutterer, unable to hide his joy, calculating that his debt with Pancho had been settled and he suddenly had something left over for some weekend fun.

The Sergeant asked for water but no one paid attention. Everyone in the pool hall was staring at him as if they were in on the joke. He felt like throwing up again, but restrained himself.

Instead, he came up with what seemed like a great idea.

In Pancho's pool hall, there are only two rules: Pay what you owe, and after that there aren't any other rules. We'll say he was crowded.

That was, in a nutshell, how it happened:

The Sergeant remembered for a moment he was a sergeant and decided to behave like one. He identified himself as National Army Sergeant XXX, representative of the Armed Forces of the Dominican Republic. Pancho identified himself as Pancho and what do I care if you're a general, ordering the pool hall doors closed with a nod of his head easily understood by the regulars. The Sergeant got stuck between tables two and three while clutching a cue stick in one hand as if it were a bat. With the other he searched in his sock for the .22 with the golden handle which had been promised to protect him from all evils.

Now it was official: the Sergeant was not going to fall into any trap easily; he'd die fighting. When they got him with the first blow from behind and his heel rolled into Pancho's hands, only the .22 remained between him and what seemed to be the beating of the century.

Some scoundrel threw a glass of beer in his eyes. The bitter, yellow liquid rolled over his face, and splashed all over on the .22.

It was soaking wet.

The gun jammed. The rest, confirmed by eyewitnesses, was, in fact, the beating of the century. The blow that finally knocked him unconscious was delivered with his own gun.

3. THE DRAGON'S DEBTS

The construction business in Santo Domingo is simple: the bosses pretend to pay the workers and the workers pretend to work. That said, it's the worker who stands to lose because, sooner or later, although always sooner rather than later, the work is finished and the money evaporates.

Pineda was the closest thing to a God when it came to building El Pancito Caliente Bakery: He was the debt collector on the project.

El Pancito Caliente would be one of the many Chinese bakeries in the capital. Unlike the others, it'd be built from scratch and wasn't part of any other restaurant/karaoke/supermarket/coffee shop/ice cream parlor like most Chinese bakeries in the city. On Saturday, June 30th, the monies arrived and thus came paychecks for the workers. This also meant paying interest and installments on Pineda's loans — at a modest rate of twenty percent per month — by the group of workers building the bakery near the La Fe expansion.

Negotiations, back payments and installments were the order of the day. Seated on a concrete block, Pineda wore a wide-brimmed hat to protect himself from the inclement one o'clock sun while he kneaded the revenues. Accompanied only by his expertise in the field, his total disdain for the working class and a small pistol whose golden handle glinted in the sun's rays, Pineda was dexterous and ruthless when it came to collecting. His reputation as a man with connections preceded him (he was the compadre of a lieutenant assigned to the president's aide de corps, and got quick access to police patrols in charge of cleaning up delinquents; in the case of Haitian defaulters, the patrol was substituted by the infamous Camiona) and thus, Pineda earned a living while losing his soul.

A clarification: Pineda worked for Tsu El Chino.

Tsu El Chino (pronounced Chu el Chino) was a dangerous guy. Not only was he behind the loans at the bakery, but he was also the owner of the bakery. Pineda had met him when he was trying to escape a nine-hundred-peso bill at a karaoke bar on Duarte Street owned by Tsu, posing as a City Hall inspector, threatening to close the business for hygiene reasons.

But if Pineda knew every trick in the book, Tsu knew the whole encyclopedia, and after getting a few good blows in, he thought better of it. He wiped the blood from his knuckles and recognized Pineda had the nerve and cool necessary to try his luck at loan sharking, an enterprise alien to his caste which had been difficult for him to get into.

Banned for six months from a betting parlor for collusion, Pineda had finally found a patron to answer to and protect.

Tsu was a short, skinny man. He was missing a finger on his left hand. Apart from being many other things, Tsu was also the boss of La Cangrena: the Chinese mafia in Santo Domingo. Disguised in cheap clothes, sharing meals and hiding burials, the members of La Cangrena walked along Duarte, Mella, 30 de Mayo and San Isidro highways without arousing the least bit of suspicion. Shielded perfectly behind polyester and motels, communicating by calligraphy and a language indecipherable to the rest of the city, these mafiosi were the silent masters of the Dominican-Chinese underworld.

Back to Pineda: On the Saturday in question, Tsu had given him orders to be more severe when collecting.

"Pinela, make'em pay, tiguele. If you can't get money for Tsu then Tsu have to find who can."

Pineda did his part, squeezing the pockets of everyone who owed him, reclaiming and pressuring like he'd never done before. By the time the next-to-last of the workers came up to pay, the bills were coming in better than expected.

The second to last in line was an individual known only as the Haitian: quiet and dark as a rotary phone; tall, with every, absolutely every muscle in his body outlined.

The building was empty. Only the Haitian and a bricklayer by the name of Montás — four weeks behind in payments — still needed to settle. Pineda was anxiously waiting for Montás' story this time, but first the Haitian.

"Haiti, let's see how we are doing," Pineda said as he went over the tattered black book. "Haiti... Haiti... here it is. Haiti... Twelve hundred and fifty before this week."

The Haitian looked more desperate than usual. His sweaty, sun-blistered face testified to a problem far bigger than he could handle.

"Let me explain ... Pinedá ... Pinedá ... next week ... next week ... this no ... this not enough."

"You see my face, you shitty Haitian?"

"Pinedá... Pinedá... I don't look bad ... next week."

"Ah, well, Pineda the chump."

"Pinedá, Pinedá... I pay, I don't look bad..."

"Of course you pay, but now. Now, Haitian! If you don't know, the truck's already on the corner."

"Pineda, Pineda... please, for Haiti... I'll pay next week... my mother is sick in Haiti, Pinedá, pol favol."

"Not next week, NOW!" He stood up and went over to the bricklayer. Tired, boiling from the heat and not having eaten at almost two o'clock in the afternoon, the worker's life seemed insignificant next to a plate of rice and a cold beer. Pineda had no time for stories.

Waiting while leaning against a wall, Montás watched with curiosity.

"C'mon, Haiti! Get me the cash now if you don't want to fuck yourself over!" Pineda pulled out the .22 caliber gold-handled pistol he carried in his belt and pointed it at the poor man.

"Pinedá, I don't have today … I pay… Monday …"

"One o'clock!"

"Pinedá … next week."

"Two o'clock …"

"Bad man, no heart, put gun down and you see." The Haitian accepted his fate and pushed out his chest, saying goodbye with dignity to a world that had mistreated him up until his last minute.

"And on three. You're fucked, Haitian!" He pulled the trigger in the same moment a bead of sweat dampened the gun barrel. The Haitian closed his eyes and Montás widened his. A stunned Pineda was going to kill the Haitian for twelve hundred pesos.

But when he pulled the trigger, the pistol clicked.

Pineda pulled several more times to no avail. He tried to hide his surprise, making believe it had all been a big joke.

"Were you scared, Haitian?" he laughed nervously, fiddling with the gun, looking around as if needing help, suspecting what might happen to him if the gun didn't respond.

But the Haitian wasn't laughing. On the contrary, he was walking slowly toward Pineda with his eyes wide open. He must have thought he was already dead. He had nothing left to lose.

"And now? What's the matter, eh, Haiti? Did you believe it? Okay, you have until tomorrow to pay, and you can just pay me half," he said, backing into the building, turning his back on the man who, in a few seconds, had become an angel of vengeance.

"Haiti, Haiti, for God's sake, it was a joke. I'm giving you a chance, Haiti, don't be an idiot." Pineda was trying to fire the gun again to no avail. "Montás? Montás, c'mere, c'mere, c'mere, c'mere!"

Montás listened, but didn't respond. *What you get, you son of a bitch, you've got it coming,* he thought.

Before he had a chance to lose himself in the construction site, the Haitian snatched the pistol from Pineda's hands and threw it at Montás.

"I don't know how to kill man with a gun … I give it to you, Motá."

With that, and with Pineda's pleas and fruitless negotiations, they disappeared into the construction site never to be seen again.

Montás caught the pistol and hid it in his pocket without even looking at it. He would have time for that later. Now he had to get out of there. He left, walking quickly towards the Tiradentes, looking around, happy for the Haitian and his debt, which would probably end up erased. "Montás, damn your mother! Help me, you asshole!" was the last thing he heard, far in the distance, as he took the sidewalk and quickened his pace.

He never looked back.

The good news for those who knew Pineda was that the rat's face made the front page of *Sucesos*, disfigured by the blows he'd received with a cinder block and stained with blood. The bad news was that Tsu lost more than forty thousand pesos and a pistol in the operation. Whoever had done in Pineda had also taken the proceeds.

Predictably, the police failed to find anything despite arresting half the neighborhood. Apparently, too many people had reason to bump off Pineda, making it impossible to single out a single person. The few suspects arrested covered for each other and, in the end, no one was found guilty.

That didn't mean Tsu didn't keep looking.

4. DOMINOS

On Wednesday nights, in the back of a Villa Juana pool hall, four guys played dominoes on a regular basis.

Occasionally, an invitation was extended to someone with enough money for the regulars to give up a seat or two at the table.

The entry fee to the game was one million pesos.

That particular night, the two hosts had guests: a pair of Chinese guys lined with bills, and with a long history of gambling.

One of the hosts, Martín the Stutterer, had met Chuíto (that was the younger guy's name) at the pool hall on Bolívar Avenue while winning three rounds at the rate of twenty thousand pesos per. Chuíto, who wasn't much of a billiard player, paid Martín from a wad of bills so big, he couldn't fit it in his wallet. As he paid, he bowed his head, smiled and thanked him. A bulb went off in Martín's head and he invited him to the billiard room in Villa Juana, where he would shower him with attention. Although grateful, Chuíto had to refuse, claiming his billiard skills weren't up to challenging him. Martín told him about the Wednesday domino game instead. Chuíto was amused to hear about the gambling and accepted the invitation, bowing his head repeatedly like a wind-up doll.

His partner was another Chinese gentleman he introduced as his dad.

The room had all the amenities of a real casino: a bar attended by a waiter who also served as scorekeeper, and giant TVs with Major League games so they could keep track of the day's bets.

The four players sat at the table and Martín simply introduced his patron as Pancho, his partner. The Chinese guys bowed their heads, Pancho made a clumsy gesture that tried to imitate them, clarified the rules of the game and shuffled the tiles: The night had begun.

Between the first and second hand, the pool hall's front door rang. The waiter opened it and returned with a thousand pesos in old and crumpled bills.

"The Sergeant paid his monthly," he said, handing the bills to Pancho, who stuffed them in his shirt pocket without counting.

The amiability lasted until the third hand. After all, what could be expected from four gangsters sitting at the same table pretending to be decent and civilized?

At the end of the fourth game, Martín and Pancho had won three by a margin of fifty points, one was a squeaker, for a total of eight hundred thousand pesos.

The fifth game was about to begin when Chuíto's dad addressed his son in Mandarin, to which Pancho immediately objected.

"Hey, Spanish, only Spanish!"

The Chinese man cut him off, mumbling through his teeth what anyone might have interpreted as a curse.

Martín the Stutterer, like a good host, intervened.

"Se-se-señores, por favor. There is no ne-ne-need," he stuttered. "We came here to play, not fight." His eyes pleaded with Pancho not to spoil the moment.

But it had been a while since the Chinese man had believed in kindness. He knew something was up.

Ninety-four to zero, the Chinese men were losing again. They weren't world champions, but they knew their business. It was their turn to shuffle. They babbled what sounded like instructions in Mandarin as they pushed the tiles to the center of the table, ready to go. Then Martín did something he'd been doing all night: He shuffled them one more time.

Martín and Pancho selected their tiles before their guests. The Chinese guys looked at each other; Tsu said something to his son. He sounded serious and determined. Just as Pancho started to protest again, the Chinese guys grabbed both him and Martín by the throat, squeezing until they almost choked. One tug and Pancho and Martin would be breathing through a new hole in their throats the size of a billiard ball.

Wasting no time, the waiter pulled a shotgun from the bar and pointed it at the Chinese guys, alternating between them.

"Let those men go right now, goddamn it!" he shouted.

"Tell him to put his gun down, otherwise say goodbye," Tsu said slowly.

"Lower the shotgun, lower the shotgun, we're going to talk," Pancho ordered with his windpipe in a lock.

The waiter nervously put down the gun and waited for instructions.

"The only thing I want is to see your tiles before you play this hand."

They had no choice. They'd been caught. Tsu pulled down Martín's tiles and Chuíto showed Pancho's. There were five fours in one hand and five twos in the other.

"Hey, this is just luck! You know who you're dealing with? Let go of me, you damned motherfucker!"

Pancho started the negotiations with a threat, to which both of the Chinese men responded by squeezing a little tighter, commenting in Mandarin and making them get up from their chairs. The waiter didn't know what to do. The Chinese guys ordered him to get out from behind the bar. Martín stuttered that this was luck, that this wasn't cheating, that if they knew what was good for them, they would let them go.

But the Chinese men remained cold and immutable. When the waiter came out from the bar and charged at them full speed, a dry kick in the throat was enough to put him out of business.

Father and son continued talking in Mandarin as the tension grew. Pancho was getting desperate. The Chinese guys told him to calm down, that everything was going to be fine.

And it was: Chuíto took a switchblade with dragon inscriptions out of his back pocket. Seeing it, Martín shouted: "Sh-sh-shit, man, wh-wh-wh-what is that thing?" Pancho swore: "You fucked up, coñazo, you already smell like dead fucking Chinese shit."

They placed Martin the Stutterer's prodigious left hand on the table while changing their grip on the throats and pointing their blades (Tsu had taken his switchblade out as well). There were screams and much confusion about the money. "Take what's on the table, just don't ever come back." But the Chinese men didn't just want the silver now. Their honor had been trampled and that couldn't be forgiven.

"Leave your hand on the table and we'll get out of this hellhole."

"Not my hand! That's my playing hand, damn you. You better kill me, or else I'll m-m-m-kill you," shouted Martín, desperate, fusing pleas and threats in a way that didn't help his case.

They forced his hand on the table, and with a sharp, forceful blow, they cut off all

five fingers of the best billiard player in the
world.

Martín fainted, Pancho screamed.

"You goddamn motherfucker, you goddamn
fucker. You guys are dead, dead!"

Tsu wiped the razor on Martín's own shirt
and put it away. He approached Pancho calmly,
staring at him, warning him about what they
shouldn't do.

"Better leave it like this, it's more conve-
nient for everyone. For your family too. But
if I find out later that there's still something
to fight about, don't think about it, I'll find
you. You don't have to look for me, don't worry."

Pancho shut his mouth.

Chuíto took the money from Martín's pockets and recovered the money given to Pancho.
Finally, they grabbed everything from the small
safe where the day's payments were kept.

More than four million pesos total.

Before leaving, Tsu took a small pistol
with a golden handle from Pancho's belt and
Chuíto took the shotgun from the waiter, who
wasn't awake anymore.

Exhausted, Pancho tried to gather his strength.

"Don't worry," he said. "One way or another, you're gonna pay for this."

The Chinese guys carefully and respectfully closed the door that led to the dangerous streets of Villa Juana.

5. ON THE WAY TO THE HOSPITAL

Getting a drunk in a car can be difficult. Getting a drunk in a car after getting hit by a car is impossible.

Puchy was lucky the cab driver actually stopped to help him.

There was no one else on the crosswalk and it would've been easy to leave him lying there on the pavement with what was clearly a broken leg, but the driver felt obligated to do the right thing and with help from the tall man with a limp, he picked him up and put him in the car.

"My leg, brother, my damn leg, men. Shit, man, shit, fuck, man. My leg, brother, my fuckin' leg..... Led Zeppelin, brother!"

Puchy had grown up affluent in Santo Domingo. Exposed to American culture of the 1970s, he hit rock bottom when he'd had to pawn his vinyl records collection in order to keep drinking. In his prime, he'd been a devoted music lover, with a marked preference for '70s hard rock as exemplified by Led Zeppelin, AC/DC and Deep Purple.

"Brother, take it easy, calm down, you crossed the street without looking the other way." The cab driver was trying get control of the situation, even as he was thinking: "Damn, and to think I was headed home in peace."

"Fuckin' shit, man. You fucked up my leg, man. Shit, brother... and, you don't have nothin' in this cab for pain, brother? A lil' bit of rum? Shit, brother, what a fucking pain, man.... Abracadabra, man!"

"Be cool, boss, calm down, we're going to take you to get checked out," said the limping man who'd helped save him. Now he was trying to give him encouragement, but Puchy wasn't having it.

"Take me, brother, take me wherever you want, Stairway to Heaven, man!"

And so, accompanied by shrieks and curses in two languages, the cab driver took off for the nearest hospital.

On their way to a hospital, Montás thought maybe someone could also check his toe, which by that time hurt as if it'd been pulverized. He peeled off his blood-soaked sock and took a minute to think about how he'd gotten here, in this cab at three o'clock in the morning, to this level of desperation given his determination to kill the president no matter what.

Montás was not the usual character in these kinds of stories.

He was a working man. In thirty-eight years, he'd done nothing but work. He'd worked as a shoeshine boy, as a laborer, as a night watchman, as a bricklayer's assistant, as a bricklayer, like an animal: work, work, work. Since he was ten years old, Montás had only known work. If it sounded redundant, it was because work had been a redundancy all his life. Montás gave up his childhood, adolescence, youth and adult life to work. And for what? For a house that was half blocks and half zinc, completely vulnerable to the whims of nature? For three children who, before the age of fifteen, had already had to leave school to join in the same cycle as their father? For a closet full of hand me downs, t-shirts with ads for hardware stores, paint and cement companies? For a submissive and supplicant smile whenever he dared to ask the boss for an advance or simply what he was entitled to?

At the end of it all were the debts. Countless debts. A tab at the grocery store and at the pawn shop. Debts to relatives and co-workers. Debts to moneylenders and *riferos*. Debts that wrapped him up and that he would never pay off. He was an intelligent man and understood he'd never have anything but debts, an old collection of Héctor Lavoe cassettes to cheer him up on Sundays and, at the end of the day, at the end of the long and dull day, darkness.

There was no light in the city. Even in the rare hours when there was light, there was still no light. That night, a desperate man thought he could bring a little light to a city where millions of blind people were walking around bumping into each other, completely in the dark.

There is nothing figurative about darkness in the above description. The only thing Montás knew for certain at the end of the day, like everyone living on this divided island, was darkness.

According to the laws of nature, eastern philosophies and holy scriptures, a decent man should be able to lead a decent life. You don't have to be a Buddha or enlightened to understand that a man who rises at five o'clock in the morning to work like a dog, who leaves his house when the sun hasn't come up and returns when it's already gone, a man whose calloused hands lift other people's fortunes, such a man should be entitled to a decent life.

But since the world had been a world, things had never been fair. Tonight things would be different, if only for a few hours. Someone had to pay. Someone had to pay. The impunity, the irresponsibility, the lack of decency, the lack of humanity in the city would come to an end with a single shot.

Who was responsible for all that? If the boss is responsible for the construction, the guy now sleeping comfortably in that mansion must be responsible for all this.

After that assertion, logical even for a bricklayer with a fourth-grade education, he had no doubts.

"Shit, brother, man, where's the clinic, bro? What a pain, man. Hotel California, man. You sleep well there, man. Air conditioning, champagne and everythin', man. Where? Man, where?... The place, man, the people at that place are gonna come look for me, man. Abracadabra, brother, abracadabra! Look, man, my old man's got dough, man, don't throw me in a hospital, man."

"Enough, brother! Shut up already!" Montás came out of his thoughts, agitated. "That's enough. Be quiet for a while, we're almost there."

While all this was going on, the cab driver was plotting to get out of this entanglement, figuring out how to leave the drunk and the loud-mouthed man trying to get to the president's house at three o'clock in the morning, to look for things he had not lost.

The hospital was dark, like the city. The cab stopped in front of the ER and the cab driver got out of the car. On the passenger side, Montás opened the back door to give him a hand.

"Easy, baby, easy. Take it easy, brother, this thing hurts like hell, man. Shit, men, the fuckin' pain, man. Abracadabra, bro."

It was a difficult task. The drunk weighed as much as a dead man. Montás took him by the arms and the driver by the legs. Montás' shirt was tucked in, revealing the golden flash of the pistol grip. The cab driver's eyes widened, stunned by what he was seeing.

They hurried to rest him on the ground. As Montás caught his breath, Mario Cabrera jumped into his cab, accelerated, burning rubber, and disappeared, turning the corner as fast as the old Hyundai could go.

And so there they were, two limping guys at the ER door of a hospital shut down at three o'clock in the morning.

Montás realized he'd fallen into a trap. Everyone knows what happens to a driver who runs over someone in this city, and the cab driver had dumped his problem on Montás.

"Say, man, he left us, that mothafucka, bro. Mothafucka!"

"Maldita madre," he said, corroborating the drunk's sentiment, but in Spanish.

No one came out of the ER. That only happens in the movies. Here you have to go in and pray to God someone who might have passed by a medical school is awake and then beg them for a stretcher and some medicine.

The drunk was leaning against Montás on his good leg. Serving as a crutch for each other, and to the tune of "mothafucka, bro, mothafucka," they went in.

The hospital ER was everything an emergency room should be: gloomy and depressing, with the smell of death lurking behind the curtains. On the other side of a pane of glass, an overweight nurse stood at attention.

"Can I help you?"

"Well, miss, man, this guy was riding in a cab that hit me, but it wasn't his fault, man. No, no, nope ... it was another mothafucka, man. But this leg, brother, I'm in such fuckin' pain, man..."

"So you ran him over..."

"No, no, excuse me," said Montás." I don't even have a license, how am I going to run him over?"

"So you were driving without a license when you ran him over ..." "Ma'am ..."

"Miss ..."

Montás was taken aback.

"Excuse me, miss, I don't even know how to drive. I was in the cab that hit this man and then left us stranded out here."

"Yeah, man, yeah. My leg is really fucked up, man, fucked up. Let's get goin' here, babe, and you hold me up, bro. Abracadabra, dude."

"Let me get this straight: You were in a cab..."

"Uh huh ..."

"That ran over this man ..."

"Uh huh ..."

"And that took off ..."

"Uh huh ..."

"Uh huh, well, you're fucked."

"I'm fucked?"

"Yes, because you are responsible for this man."

"Didn't you hear that I wasn't driving?"

"But you were in the cab ..."

"Yes."

"So who else is going to testify other than you?"

Montás had nothing else to say. He'd wait until the authorities arrived and decided what to do with him.

In the meantime, the president was saved from his fate. For now.

In the waiting room, lying in a chair, a half-attended patient watched the scene. He looked like something out of a street fight: an arm covered by a tourniquet, bandages and dried blood everywhere. Like all criminals, his gaze was suspicious and watchful. Every time the drunk came out with something, the wounded man smiled.

New patient arrivals in an ER are like the lottery: You have to be prepared for anything. A simple heart attack can come through the door just as a mangled motorcyclist is brought in. The comedy routine between the drunk and the bricklayer was not only bizarre, but it eased the possibility of tragedy that swarms in hospitals around the world.

The injured man rose from his chair, reached for a pack of cigarettes from his pocket and walked toward the door. On the way he brushed past the new arrivals. The bricklayer instinctively tucked in his shirt, protecting what little he had on him, but the wounded man had already seen what he had to see. Nervous, he dropped the cigarettes and went out to the parking lot. He thought twice before making the call he was about to make. If he was wrong, an innocent man would die.

6. BIRDS OF PREY

How and when it all started is difficult to ascertain, but nothing suggested a happy ending.

Legend has it that, in a game of dominoes, Pancho the Rascal lost ten million pesos and Martín the Stutterer lost five fingers on one hand. A couple of Chinese guys were responsible for putting them in their place for cheating. Pancho was saved because he managed to seriously wound them before they could kill him. The Chinese guys fled and the rest … well, the rest has yet to unfold. The only certainty is that, on the street, you never need the whole story. A name or a face that leads to finding the sons of bitches is more than enough for the scoundrels to do their job.

In this case, in addition to names and faces, there was a gun.

No one could find them.

The notorious Chinese duo had evaporated like gas, and although the amount of money Pancho offered for the slightest clue was enough for any informer to open his mouth, no one had come forth in six months.

Motels and restaurants along the Duarte were constantly watched by Martín and his people, who was now known as Martin the Snipped. Never, not even once, did he get even a hint of Tsu or his son. In his uneducated views, all Chinese people looked alike and none said a word. They were where they'd started: at zero.

That's how La Cangrena worked. Effective, ruthless and, above all, silent.

"I hope you're at least dying to wake me up at three in the morning, you pussy."

"Better than that. The gun ... "

"What gun?"

"The gun, the Chinese gun ... "

"What about it?"

"A guy, a guy ran over some drunk and he's got one that might be yours, the one we took from the sergeant."

"Listen to me, listen to me real good ... if you make me get out of this bed for bullshit, I'm going to tear your head off."

"Pancho, I'm pretty sure it's the one."

After asking for the name of the hospital, and making sure the idiot didn't move from there, Pancho got dressed and left to settle his pending account.

On the corner, a cab driver made a call to a motel from a pay phone. "Buenas noches, 'El Gutico' Cabins," answered an Asian voice on the other end.

"Hello, it's El Chino."

"Which one?"

"El Chino, damnit, the cabbie."

"Ah, yes, what's up, Chino ..."

"Is Chuíto there?"

"Chuíto is picking up a payment from some guy who thought they could sneak six people into a single .... Ah, wait a sec, he's here."

"Hello?"

"Hey, it's El Chino."

"Which one?"

"El Chino, damnit, the cabbie."

"Ah, what's going on, Chino."

"The gun, Chuíto. A guy I just dropped off at the hospital has the gun."

"Pineda's pistol?"

"That one."

"You sure?"

"Sure enough. We were giving a ride to a drunk I ran down and his shirt got untucked. I saw the handle and it's yours, man, for sure. That guy's the double crosser."

Since motel owners don't sleep, Chuíto just had to knock on the door of the office next door and Tsu was made aware of the situation. Within minutes they were out with a couple of ninety-pound thugs looking for the man with the gun who'd killed Pineda, and who had brought the police to their door, but more importantly, who had stolen their money.

Miraculous as it may seem, Puchy's father really was wealthy.

"Does he have insurance?" the nurse asked.

"Yeah, baby, insurance." He pulled out a blue Velcro wallet that once read AC/DC on the outside. Its only content was a very prestigious insurance card that, fortunately, the hospital accepted

Indeed, Puchy's dad, despite having completely disowned him, had protected him with the best health insurance in the country. He knew, given the conditions in which his son roamed the streets, he'd need it often, and he saw it as a kind of investment rather than a bequest.

Montás thought several times about running, but his own decency, his limp and the nurse's threat convinced him to stay. He decided, in the absence of insurance like the drunkard's, to try to convince an intern to x-ray his toe.

Just as Montás was listening to the last rejection of the night, a hail of gunfire shattered the calm. Outside, only a few steps away, automatic weapons blasted away, running and breathlessness rocked the night. Everyone in the ER dropped to the floor and Puchy peed his pants.

"Shit, man, fuckin' shit. We went down the Stairway to Heaven, brother," he said, wiping the hot stuff rolling down his pants with his hands.

The shooting lasted almost five minutes. Screams of pain were interspersed with insults and pleas for help. Everything could be heard as if it were happening in the room and above them. They clutched their heads and squatted down, seeking shelter under furniture and chairs, praying and asking God to get them out of there alive.

When silence finally fell, more than ten men lay dead in the parking lot, half of them Chinese, the rest locals. A stocky dark-haired

man with a fucker's face and a white man
with five fingers missing from his left hand
lay dying among the locals. Montás came out
with the .22 in his hand, as if he could defend
himself with that. He'd never seen anything
like this in his life and never would again. He
didn't know any of the men on the ground,
nor did he understand anything.

He scanned the parking lot, looking for clues
as to what had happened, unaware he carried
in his hands the only clue that mattered.

What exactly happened outside, no one
will ever know. The legend will be told the
way it wants to be told. Everything pointed
to a settling of scores in which both sides
knew how to shoot. The police were content
to report that ten criminals would no longer
be stalking the streets of the city. Ten people
who weren't supposed to get together had
gotten together. There are those who say there
are no coincidences and everything is fated
without our awareness until it's all resolved.

The only ones left alive, although in agony,
were the dark-haired man with the fucker's

face and one of the Chinese men, the oldest. Both caught a glimpse of Montás with the pistol in his hand, and both sighed the same thing, albeit in different languages.

"The pistol."

And with that, they died.

For a change, the police didn't take long getting there. Despite the fact that it was three in the morning, a crowd had gathered in a matter of minutes. Some recognized Pancho or Martín, and others asked who the Chinese guys were.

While all this was going on, Montás managed to slip away and leave the night's madness behind.

7 . HOME

Montás walked away from the scene, determined to get home. Someone up in heaven seemed to be sending him signals. His head and his intentions had cooled.Night was giving way to an orange dawn. He shuffled his feet to Máximo Gómez street. His toe hurt less now. He pulled out the pistol and examined it. He realized that he, like the Haitian, wouldn't know how to kill with a gun either.

He threw it away in the next garbage can he passed. He raised his head just at the moment when a line of cars with sirens passed him at full speed. It was the president's motorcade, on its way to the National Palace.

He thought he saw The Man sitting in the car with license plate number 01. He thought he recognized him, with his fat spectacles and balding head, just like he appeared in newspapers and on billboards, smiling and optimistic. He could have sworn the sonofavitch had waved at him.

When he walked in the door, Esther was waiting for him, asleep in an old armchair in the living room. Montás woke her with a tender kiss on the forehead, and Esther hugged him.

When she asked him where he'd been, Montás said no one could sleep in that heat, and that he'd gone for a walk. He took off his shirt and told her he was going to take a shower. Esther said there was no water and the electricity hadn't been on for the last twenty hours. On his way to the bathroom, Montás stopped for a moment, nodded his head in disbelief and smiled bitterly.

Esther hugged him from behind and kissed his back. The sun had risen and was streaking through a window. She whispered that if they'd had gas she would've made him a little breakfast, a little herring with bananas, but instead she was going to make him a little cheese sandwich to take to the construction site, even if it wasn't hot.

Montás kissed her hand and closed his eyes. Things were not going to be all right, they would never be all right. His moment had passed. From now on he would settle quietly. He would work so he could walk this earth that seemed to hate him and he'd never complain again.

Although from time to time, in the heat of the twelve o'clock sun, while he sweated like an animal making millionaires richer, as he realized somewhere in Santo Domingo the Man was still shitting on his hard work, just like all those before him, and like all those who would follow; at that moment he cursed the cab driver who ran over that damned drunkard and didn't let him go and fix things for everyone, once and for all.

INDEX